Golden
TOP SHELF
An imprint of Torquere Press Publishers
PO Box 2545
Round Rock, TX 78680
Copyright 2013 by Sean Michael
Cover illustration by BSClay
Published with permission
ISBN: 978-1-61040-441-9

www.torquerepress.com

First Torquere Press Printing: February 2013
Printed in the USA

**If you enjoyed Golden,
you might enjoy these Sean Michael titles:**

Bent

Gravity

Personal Best

Secrets, Skin and Leather

The Velvet Glove Series

Golden

Golden
by Sean Michael

Torquere
Press
Inc.
romance for the rest of us
www.torquerepress.com

Golden

Chapter One

Justin sat on the edge of his balcony, feet swinging, a half drunk bottle of bourbon in one hand, his gold medal in the other. He could see the swimming pool, two stories down, and he wondered, not for the first time, if he would hit the water if he jumped.

There was a party going on behind him, people dancing and laughing, celebrating the Fourth of July. There were fireworks going off in the night sky, blue and red and green and white and...

God, it wasn't supposed to be this way. It wasn't supposed to be empty and lonely and... He wasn't supposed to be worthless. He wasn't supposed to be sitting on his balcony and thinking about jumping. Was he?

"Jase? Honey? You okay?" Somebody whose name he didn't know came out, smiled at him.

"No. No. I'm just watching." *Go away, leave me alone. Let me sit here.*

He let the medal swing, the gold catching the light from the tiny explosions. It took a minute, but the little girl disappeared back into the apartment. He was so tired of lying. So tired of fucking everything.

He pulled his phone out of his pocket, opened it and dialed one on speed dial. *Please, Coach. Just answer the phone. I know you don't have to, but please...*

"Chris Jarvis."

His eyes closed at the familiar voice, and suddenly he couldn't speak.

"Hello?" He could picture Coach frowning as he said it, moving to check the call display, which Coach never did when he first answered. "Just, that you?"

"Yeah. Yeah. I. Hey, Coach." *I miss you.*

"Hey, Justin." Was it his imagination, or did Coach's voice get warmer? "How's it going?"

"It's..." He looked out at the pool again. He could probably make it. "It's going. Happy July."

Chris chuckled. "Happy July, kid. Feels odd, doesn't it?"

"Yeah. Yeah, it does." Everything did. Everything. "I didn't mean to bother you."

"If it was a bother, I wouldn't have answered the phone."

"Yeah." Chris hadn't answered the phone for the better part of a year, really, telling him it was time to move on. He'd retired, with four gold medals, two silvers and a bronze and, after two Olympic Games, hundreds of competitions, thousands of races, and five shoulder surgeries, he was done.

No more sponsors. No more early morning practices. No more someone worrying about him. It was just this apartment and a job designing web sites for a shoe company.

"You watching the fireworks?" At least Chris wasn't in a hurry to get him off the phone.

"I'm on my balcony. You?"

"On the TV over the capital." He could almost hear Coach's self-deprecating smile. "I was thinking of heading out for a midnight snack."

"You always loved midnight pancakes." They'd eaten more syrup at one a.m...

"Like you hated our midnight snack attacks. The Denny's on Maple is open all night."

"I'm... I've been drinking, Coach. I can't drive down." Wait. Had Chris invited him?

"I'll swing by and get you. Those pancakes are calling my name."

"I... I'll be downstairs."

"See you in ten." Coach cut the line.

Justin slipped off the balcony ledge, heading through crowd in his apartment without a word. His roommates would deal. It wasn't until he was all the way downstairs and waiting before he thought to wonder how Coach knew where he lived.

Chris pulled up in front of the apartment complex where Justin lived, sure enough, there the man was, lounging against the side of the building. He waved, engine idling.

Tall and blond, the all-American looks marred only by the red nose that proved that there'd been too much drinking—Justin came over, smiling crookedly. "Coach."

"Hey, kid. Get on in." He smiled, let himself admire a little. Justin wasn't his swimmer anymore; he was allowed to notice.

Justin slid in, buckled up, those blue eyes on him. "How's it going?"

"It's going. How about you?" He pulled back out into the road, headed for the all-night Denny's.

"I..." He could hear Justin's swallow. "It's going."

Uh-huh. Drinking, calling him out of the blue. It wasn't going great, if he was any judge. And when it came to Justin, he was. He'd had to be a hard-ass with Justin after retirement, simply because the kid needed to find his way. Chris hadn't been angry when Justin announced his retirement. The kid had gone from the games to surgery and had spent months just rehabbing. It had been the right time for Justin.

Chris knew he'd never train anyone as talented as Justin again—lightning didn't strike twice—but he enjoyed his job coaching kids at the Santa Barbara Swim Club. There were a couple who might even do well at Nationals in a few years. If they stuck with it.

"You still doing web-design?" he asked.

"Yep. Shoes. Everybody needs shoes."

"You sound so excited about it." He pulled into the restaurant parking lot.

"I'm a grown up now. I don't get to be excited anymore." Justin winked at him.

Now that wasn't right; someone needed to show Justin how to be excited again. That he wanted it to be him, had always wanted it to be him, didn't change how much Justin needed.

"Have you found the next great swimmer?" Justin asked.

"Nope. I've seen a lot of kids with potential, though. There's one or two at the club who could be pretty good if they put the work in." It took way more than just talent to win; dedication and passion were even more important than ability. Justin had always been great at putting his head down and working hard.

"Bummer. You deserve to have the greatest."

"I have the greatest." He reached out and squeezed Justin's shoulder. "Come on, conversation's always better over pancakes."

"Yeah. Syrup. Bacon. Coffee." Those pretty eyes were bloodshot as fuck.

He was going to have to do something about that, about Justin's drinking, the attitude. He might have said it wasn't his place anymore, but Justin had called him. And he wasn't the man's coach any longer, and that opened a whole world of possibilities.

They went in and the hostess took them to a booth. Justin sat, slid over, all wrapped in himself. So Chris sat in next to him instead of across from him. Those pretty blue eyes flashed over at him, surprised. How many times had he seen that? He raised an eyebrow, waited patiently for Justin to vocalize his thoughts.

"I've missed you."

That made him smile, and he nodded, put his hand on Justin's leg. "Yeah, I've missed you, too."

Justin offered him a half grin, then sighed softly. "So before I interrupted, what were you up to tonight?"

"I was watching the fireworks over the capital on TV and contemplating an early night, although the pancakes were also calling my name. You sounded like you had a party going on."

"There was a party at the apartment. My roommate's friends."

He smiled at the waitress as she came up to their table. "Two Grand Slams with pancakes, eggs scrambled with cheese, bacon and sausages, two coffees and a tall glass of milk, please."

"You remembered." Justin sounded surprised.

"Of course I remembered." He'd been Justin's coach for years. Four years not being there wasn't going to wipe out what came before.

"Do you think... Do you think it ever gets better?"

He frowned. "Do I think what's getting better? Be specific, Just."

"Everything." Justin looked at him, eyes just lost. "Is this really it? I've like, had my good stuff and it's just this, forever?"

Jesus, that lost look slayed him.

"You need to find new good stuff, kid. There's more to life than swimming and gold medals."

"Is this the first time you've ever said those words?"

He had to laugh at that. "I know. For most of your life that's all that's been important, isn't it?" He rubbed Justin's leg. "Now that you have those gold medals in your back pocket? There's more to life."

"Yeah." Justin nodded, offered him a fake smile and then took his coffee from the waitress.

Chris snorted, but thanked the waitress and added sugar to his own coffee. When she'd left he turned back to Justin. "Don't give me that look, Just. I know what a real smile looks like on you and that ain't it."

Justin put sugar in his coffee, then shrugged. "It doesn't matter. Tell me about your swimmers."

"You should come see them. I could use an assistant coach, and it's in the budget." It was, he thought, one of his better ideas. He'd refused to let Justin lean on him when the kid had retired because it would have been so easy to just become Justin's lover and that wasn't right. He would have felt like he was running Justin's life. Justin had called him, though, had reached out after four years. That was enough waiting time, right?

Justin shook his head. "I'm no coach. Are they any good?"

"Come with me on Saturday and see for yourself," Chris insisted.

"Maybe. I don't know."

"But I do. You're coming."

Justin looked at his coffee. "Maybe."

He nudged his leg against Justin's, waiting for those eyes to turn to him. "You're coming."

Justin changed the subject. "Tell me about your life now. I know it's different."

"It is. I have a lot more free time I don't know what to do with."

"You should find someone amazing." The words were sad.

"I already did." And maybe he'd been too quick to push Justin out of the nest. He'd had to, though, had to send Justin out into the world. Didn't mean he couldn't welcome the kid back into the nest again, though. Hell, not answering the phone that first year had been the hardest thing he'd ever done and he'd always gone back and forth in his head, had to convince himself it was the right thing to do.

"Yeah? You competing with him?"

He chuckled softly, leaned against Justin. "I'm taking about *you*."

"Dork. I'm a has-been." Justin wasn't the kind of kid that was a spokesperson or a commentator. He just wanted to swim, not play the game.

"You're not competing anymore, that doesn't make you a has-been." It made him a little mad, the way Justin was deflated.

"Food's here." Justin unwrapped his silverware.

"If you finish first, you can have half my pancakes." Like they used to do.

"Like my old ass needs your pancakes." Justin patted his belly.

"You're still looking pretty damn good." He was allowed to notice now, allowed to admire. And admire he did.

"Thanks. It took a few months to figure out the whole food thing."

"Yeah, you have to eat like the rest of us when you aren't training twelve hours a day."

He definitely wanted Justin at the practice on Saturday. Let the kids see what a true champion looked like, what it took.

"Yeah." Justin sighed softly.

"Stop that."

"Stop what?" Justin moved his eggs around the plate.

"Getting down on yourself. Just because you're not still competing doesn't mean life is over."

"No. No, it's not." Justin looked at him. "I wish it was, sometimes."

He grunted. Fuck. Had he made the right decision four years ago? He had to believe the answer was yes. "No. It's not and you promise me right now if you ever feel like that, you give me a call."

"I did."

And he'd answered. Go them for getting that right at least.

"Come home with me tonight."

"I don't..." Justin looked at him, so sad. "You aren't my coach anymore. I can't come home."

"I'm not asking as your coach, Justin." He put his hand back on Justin's thigh, squeezed. God, those muscles were still so strong.

Chris leaned in, holding Justin's gaze as he brought their lips together. Justin's eyes went wide, huge, staring at him. He pressed their lips together, kissed Justin. Damn, but Justin's lips were soft and warm and he wanted more. He'd wanted this man for years, wanted to know how that body felt hard and hot and aching for him.

He slid his tongue along the seam of Justin's lips. Come on, Justin, open up.

For the longest second, Chris didn't think he was going to, then Justin made this harsh, desperate sound, kissing him hard. He kissed back, taking control of the kiss to devour Justin's mouth. Justin tasted like booze and coffee and tears. *No more. God damn it.*

He cupped Justin's head, tilting it slightly so he could deepen the kiss. Then he let their lips drift apart and he leaned back, smiled.

"I... I gotta go. I need to. Let me out." Justin's eyes were huge.

"No, Justin. You don't. You need to stay and eat and then come home with me."

"I need out." There was the hint of pure panic on Justin's face.

"Look at me, Just." He held Justin's face between his hands. "Look at me and breathe." Justin knew this, knew how to breathe with him.

Justin sucked in a breath, another, and then Justin was with him.

"We're a good team, Justin. It's about time we started acting like it."

"What? We're not a team, not anymore."

"I think it's about time we were one again, though. Don't you?" He pressed their lips together again.

"Coach. We're in a Denny's."

He blinked and chuckled. "Yeah, I guess we are. Eat up, I know you're hungry." He didn't regret the kiss, though. He didn't regret his words, either.

"A little." Justin started eating, shoveling it in. The man was as tight and muscled as always, so he had to be working out. Justin just needed something more fulfilling than designing websites to do. Chris had just the thing, too.

He dug into his own food, being sure to leave half his pancakes on his plate. He noticed that Justin left him one piece of sausage and a piece of bacon, too. When he was finished with everything else, he traded plates with Justin and they happily ate each other's leftovers. It was like old times.

Only better because he was taking Justin home. To his bed.

Chapter Two

What was he doing? Justin sat in Chris' car, heading toward the house he'd called home for years. What was he doing?

"This is a good thing, Just."

"Is it? For you?" He gnawed on his lower lip.

"For both of us. I wouldn't do this just for me."

"I just... I'm... two hours ago I was standing on my balcony." Thinking about jumping into the pool.

"Drinking and getting yourself worked up enough you called me."

"I wanted to hear your voice." Needed to, maybe.

"I'm glad you called. I've missed you a lot." They turned onto the street where Coach lived.

"Why didn't you call?" Why did you tell me to go and that I couldn't come back?

"Because it wouldn't have been right to put you in my bed and keep you. You had to find your own way in the world." They pulled into the garage and Coach shut off the engine, turned to him. "I wasn't going to take advantage of you, Just."

"Take advantage? I was twenty-three. I wasn't a kid. You were my home, man."

"I was your coach, I told you what to do every day and then I wasn't your coach anymore and it wasn't my place. You think I did the wrong thing? You think what

I did tonight I should have done right after you retired?"

"I don't know. I don't..." He got out of the car, went to hit the garage door opener to close it. He needed to go home. Think.

Coach climbed out and looped an arm around his waist, let him into the house. "I did the right thing, Just. You didn't even know if you were into me or not. You needed to go out and see what else the world had to offer."

"I..." Wait. Wait, he'd been...

Coach tilted his head and stole his breath with another kiss. The man had to stop this. Really. Later.

Justin's cock was achingly hard, and the kisses were perfect.

The kiss went deeper, Coach bending him back over one strong arm. He held on, the room swimming behind him. The kiss went on and on, totally stealing his breath. His body was aching, his prick hurting he was so hard. Coach's hand slid from his neck on down, all the way down to his waistband.

Please. Fuck, please. He just needed to come.

Then Coach's hand drifted down the rest of the way, cupping and squeezing him through his jeans. He bucked up, humping fast. His body had wanted this for so long. Groaning, Coach pushed him up against the wall, free hand working on his belt, his button.

"Want." He growled the word against Coach's lips. "Please."

"Come on." Coach grabbed his hand and dragged him toward the bedroom.

Justin nodded, following along fast enough that they were almost running.

"Naked," growled Coach, pulling off his own t-shirt and then working on his jeans.

"Uh-huh." He stepped out of his shorts, shrugged the button-up off.

Once he was naked, his hard prick hard pointed right at Coach's cock, which was pointing right back. Coach grabbed his arms and tugged him close, bringing their mouths together again. He reached down, wrapped his fingers around their cocks and started jerking them off.

"This time," muttered Coach. "But then we do it right."

"Uh-huh." Whatever. He needed.

Coach kissed him again, one hand wrapping around his, speeding his movements. They jacked fast and hard, driving together like they'd done this forever. Their kisses made everything better, hotter. His balls drew up and he went up on tiptoe, so close.

"Come for me, Just. Right now."

"Right..." Heat poured from him and he groaned, moaning his coach's name.

"Fuck, yes, Just." Coach bucked, cock pushing through their hands and more slick sprayed, coating their fingers.

Oh. Oh, better.

Coach moaned softly, rubbed their noses together. "God, I've wanted to do that forever."

Justin took a deep breath, trying to find his feet. The smell of them together filled his nose as he breathed, and then Coach rubbed a hand on his belly, marking him with their combined come. His muscles rippled and rolled, and he couldn't help his groan.

"The things I want to do to you, Just. I want to turn you inside out and make you mine."

"Don't tease." He'd wanted to be Chris' long before now.

"I'm not teasing, Just. I mean it."

"I'm not... What are we doing here?"

"We're giving into the feelings we suppressed for a lot of years. We have something here between us." Coach tugged Justin down onto the mattress as he spoke.

Coach's bed was soft, warm—not at warm as Chris, the man's body was like a flame. Those amazing lips landed on his again, this kiss long and slow, but no less intense. Coach's hands were on his head, on his ass, drawing him so that they were touching everywhere.

He'd always liked Coach's hands, but they'd never touched him like this before. It was kind of stunning. It was dizzying. Crazy-making. Perfect.

One hand slipped between them, Coach going for his nipples, touching lightly, and then harder. The sting made his gasp, made him grab Coach's hand. Coach chuckled and did it again.

"Stings." He groaned the word into Coach's lips.

"Makes your cock twitch." Coach twisted his nipple this time.

"S...so?" He arched, rubbed.

"So you like it. And I'm going to keep doing it." Coach proved that by twisting the other one.

"No way." He groaned, tried to push Coach over.

Coach pushed *him* over, rolling on top of him and straddling him, his arms held together on his belly in just one of Coach's. "Are you always this pushy in bed?" Coach asked.

"I don't usually fuck in a bed." He was more the quick hand job in the showers guy.

"You will now. Bed's the best place for it. Though there's something to be said for testing out the rest of the furniture in the house."

God, Coach was strong. "I..."

Coach leaned in and kissed him again, long and slow and almost devastating. By the time Coach's lips left his, he was spinning. Dazed. Needy.

"Pick a word, Just. Pick a word that means stop no matter where we are, no matter what we're doing."

Golden

"Like when we were swimming? Like redlight?" They'd done that so Coach would know if it was serious—a cramp, something more than just bitching.

Coach nodded, looked pleased. "Exactly like that."

"Can't that it be it?"

"Yeah, I don't see why not." Coach leaned in and kissed him again. "That way you won't forget it."

He nodded. "Are we going in the pool?"

"Not right now. We can later." Coach drew the fingers of his free hand along Justin's chest, his rib cage, his belly.

It was like he was Alice and this was Wonderland.

Bending, Coach wrapped hot lips around his right nipple, drawing it in and sucking hard. His hands were still trapped between them, his wrists wrapped in Coach's strong grip.

"You'll leave a mark!" Oh, god. The ache. He wanted to scream, it was so good.

Coach's reply was to bite, teeth sinking into the hard point. His mouth opened, his body stiffening, too surprised to do anything. Coach soothed the hurt with flicks of his tongue, then went back to sucking strongly. His entire nipple was going to be purple, maybe even the pale skin around it would be.

"I. I. I." He was jabbering, confused, lost.

Letting go of his nipple, Coach's mouth covered his, swallowing his sounds. The kisses made things easier, better, and suddenly he could breathe again.

Coach played with his nipple with a single finger, pushing against it and making it ache, the bruise left behind super sensitive. He whimpered into Coach's lips, so confused, so turned on. His other nipple tingled, ached in a totally different way.

He wiggled, moaned, and he'd rub it, but his hands were caught. Coach's fingers slipped away from his right nipple, moving to push into his hip. It was bright and sharp.

Just looked at Coach, confused. "What..."

"Deep sensation, Just. Feel everything." Coach's hand slid slowly toward his unabused nipple.

"I am. I am." His heart started pounding harder.

Coach's gaze held his, the tension increasing as those fingers inched closer.

"I. Don't." He couldn't be patient.

Coach just held his gaze, fingers moving even slower, if that was possible. He couldn't breathe. He was freaking out. He tugged at Coach's hands, frowning when the grip held. When Coach got to his nipple, those fingers didn't pinch or twist or tweak it. They didn't even touch it. Instead, Coach circled the pink skin surrounding his nipple, teasing terribly.

"Coach..." Justin needed... something.

Coach grinned, finger flicking across the hard tip of his nipple. The little zing was weird, huge, and he pulled away, jerked away. Coach followed, finger flicking across his nipple again. The fingers around his wrists tightened, reminding him that he was caught.

"Stop it. I'm going home." His heart was racing.

"You are home, J." Coach pinched his nipple this time, making it ache like the other one.

He twisted again, beginning to fight. "Stop teasing me!"

"Tell me what sex usually is for you. Tell me what you've done, what you haven't done but want to." Coach's fingers slipped over his nipple again, then again.

"I... Hand jobs in the showers. You know. Maybe a couple of quickies in the bathroom at a club."

"Define quickies." Coach flicked his nipple twice, then dragged all his fingers over it. Almost like a reward for his answer.

"Huh? You mean, like, what did we do?"

"Yes, that's what I mean."

There was no touch to his nipple this time.

"Just rubbing off in a stall, maybe a blowjob. Drunk stuff."

Coach pinched his nipple, gave it a tweak. "No penetration?"

"No." It hadn't come up. It wasn't like he was out, for fuck's sake. His roommate thought he was straight.

"Good." Leaning down, Coach wrapped hot lips around the nipple, sucking hard.

"Coach!" He pushed his hands down, bringing his fingers and Coach's toward his cock.

"Pushy, pushy." Coach bit his nipple, then slapped it with that hot tongue.

"Fuck!" They struggled together again, moaning as Justin tried to get the upper hand.

Coach's hand tightened around his wrists, pushing them into his belly as those hot lips tightened around his skin, sucking hard again. Fuck, he was going to be bruised. Justin yelled, the sound leaving some space inside him to breathe. Coach hummed, like he approved of the shout, hand squeezing his wrists for a moment.

Panting, sweating, Justin felt like he'd been working out. Letting his nipple go, Coach raised his head and blew across his wet skin. Justin gasped, a rush of pleasure flooding him.

Smiling, Coach held his gaze again as he reached between them to jack his prick. Twice.

Justin shot hard enough he bit his tongue.

Coach let go of his hands and rubbed the come into his belly. Slowly his breath slowed, his heart rate easing back. Coach rubbed their noses together, then their cheeks. Justin started to relax, feeling safer than he had in years.

"Love you, J."

"Liar." He cuddled into Chris' throat. The lie, though, felt good and he'd take it.

Chapter Three

C hris was having the best dream ever. Ever. He was wrapped around Justin, his boy's body warm and perfect against him.

"Mmm..." He nuzzled into Justin's neck.

"Coach." Justin stretched, body sliding against his.

This was the most real dream he'd ever had. He slid his hand along Justin's skin, eyes popping open. This wasn't a dream. The night before came rushing back to him and he groaned , pushed closer.

"Shh. Sleeping." Justin petting him, hand sliding over his arm.

He chuckled, nuzzling into Justin's neck, licking. God, Justin tasted good. He'd been dreaming of this for years, of this sweet body naked, against him. He licked his way along Justin's neck, over Justin's jaw and to those sweet lips. Justin moaned, lips parting for him. He pushed in, tasting Justin's mouth, moaning into the heat.

Justin's eyes popped open, looking at him. "Coach."

Chris slid his hand around Justin's waist and tugged him closer. "Hey, J."

"I... it wasn't a dream."

"No, not a dream." It was real. They were real.

"Wow." Justin blinked, staring at him. "We're naked."

"And in bed. With each other."

"Yeah. We came a lot."

He chuckled. "We're making up for all those years we didn't come at all."

Justin smiled at him, the look unsure. He wasn't having any of that. He slipped a finger across one of Justin's nipples, knowing they'd be sensitive this morning. Justin pulled away, hands protecting the bruised bits.

"No hiding from me." He grabbed Justin's hands and tugged them away.

"But... They ache."

"Good." That's what he wanted. Sensation and awareness from this beautiful man.

"Good?"

"Yep. Very good." He pinched one of Justin's nipples, Justin's prick jerking hard against his thigh.

"Don't." Justin's wrists twisted in his hands.

He deliberately tweaked the other nipple.

"Don't!" Justin turned away from him.

"Where are you going?"

"I don't know."

Chuckling, he pulled Justin back up to him. "I think we should start with a few ground rules." Justin had always responded so well to rules; it would translate beautifully to the bedroom, to their new relationship.

"Rules?"

"Yep. You're familiar with those." Chris contemplated a good place to start.

"For training, yeah." Justin looked at him. "I'm not sure what's going on here."

"We're giving in to our baser urges, Just. We're doing what we've wanted to do for years. You need rules, structure, love."

"You don't love me. You loved being with a winner, and I'm not one anymore."

"Why don't you believe I love you?" He'd spent years telling himself he couldn't have what he wanted with

Justin no matter how much he loved the man. Now he could. Now they both could.

"If I hadn't called last night, you wouldn't have even thought of me."

"I've thought of you every day since you retired."

"Bullshit."

"It's the truth, Justin." He met the man's eyes, let Justin read the truth there.

"You need a swimmer to take care of."

"No, J. I need you to take care of." He thought maybe just doing it would prove it to Justin. He hoped so anyway.

Justin looked confused, but didn't argue.

"Rule number one. You don't touch your cock without my permission."

"What? It's my cock."

That was the hottest thing he'd ever seen, the way J's lips parted.

"And I'm in charge. Rule number two is you don't get to run yourself down. Ever." He didn't ever want to hear Justin say another negative thing about himself. Ever.

"I'm not... what's going on?" Justin's cock was filling, rapidly.

"It's called BDSM, Justin. I'm the Dom—the coach—and you're the sub—the one who has my focus. I lay down the rules, just like you're used to, only instead of being about swimming, it's about us." There was no way he could have done this until he was no longer Justin's coach and Justin came to him. Thank god, Justin finally had.

"What's the point? There's no point to anything anymore."

It made him growl, to hear how lost Justin was. "The point is that I love you enough to make you happy again."

"If you loved me, you wouldn't have waited to call me, to see me. You would have missed me." Justin pulled away from him, sliding off the bed.

"Get your ass back here."

"Make me. I'm not your swimmer anymore." Justin sounded stubborn, petulant.

"Get. Your. Ass. Back. Here."

"Fuck you, asshat." Justin flipped him off.

Oh, he didn't think so. He climbed out of bed and grabbed hold of Justin's arm before the man could even blink. "You don't flip me off." He dragged Justin over to his dresser, started looking for cuffs.

"Let me go!" Justin was still so strong.

"No." He found a pair of leather cuffs and he grabbed them, showed them to Justin.

"What the hell? You're, like, kinky?"

"Have you never heard of BDSM?" He put the cuffs on Justin's wrists in front of him.

"You mean like whip me, beat me, make me write bad checks?"

"That's one kind. I've never picked up a whip in my life and I don't plan to start. With you and me, it's all about control." He picked up Justin's hands. "You flipped me off. Your punishment is loss of your hands for the day."

"What? Punishment? What the fuck?"

"You don't do as you're told, you disrespect me and you get a punishment. And don't tell me it's not fair because you didn't know. You were looking for a fight; you were looking for a reaction when you flipped me off. Congratulations, you got it." He cupped Justin's face and made sure those eyes were looking into his. "I see you, Justin. I *see* you."

"I have to go. I have to."

"No." He leaned in and kissed Justin to keep more protests silent.

Justin was shaking, embarrassed and turned on and sad.

When the kiss ended, he leaned their foreheads together. "You're mine, Justin. All of you."

"I'm scared."

"Of what?" He needed Justin to open up to him.

Justin sighed. "Everything."

"You don't have to face any of it alone anymore."

"Until you get bored or tired or..."

"That's not going to happen." He dragged Justin back to bed. Maybe he'd made a mistake, letting this go so long; but how could he have done this when he was still Justin's coach? They were done now, though. No more separation. He was going to give Justin what they both needed.

"You can't just put handcuffs on me and keep me."

Sure he could. "Watch me." He pushed Justin down onto the bed, followed.

Just like when they'd started training in the pool, Justin looked at him, moved him.

He brought their mouths together. "I love you and I'm going to take care of you and I'm going to keep saying it until you believe it."

"I wanted to jump yesterday. See if I could make the pool from the balcony."

Jesus. He'd known that, but hearing it again made his whole body clench for a long moment. "I'm glad you called me instead."

"I just wanted to talk to you."

"Good." He'd come close to losing his boy forever. He wasn't going to take that chance again. Ever.

He kissed Justin, gently this time, just so he could feel his boy. He could taste Justin, too, the booze gone now. Justin slowly relaxed for him, opened for him. He pressed their bodies together, Justin's hands trapped between them.

Needy man. Chris wanted him, so badly. He couldn't

wait to sink into the perfect heat of his boy's body. The virgin heat of his boy's body. Groaning, he deepened the kiss. Justin opened for him, eyes focused, on him. He drew his hand down along Justin's breastbone. Justin took a deep breath, body moving under his hand.

"So fucking sexy, Just."

Justin's cheeks pinked. So pretty.

Humming, he kissed Justin again, taking his time to explore. Justin had bulked up, more muscular now, broader in the chest. His fingers mapped his boy, discovered every new change, and every inch he already knew by sight.

"I don't swim anymore. It's weird."

That surprised him. One of the reasons why Justin had been so good was how much he loved the water. "Why not?"

"It's just weird. People look at me."

"Expecting a show? I can get you in a pool where you'll be unobserved, J."

"Yeah?" Oh, there was a hint of hunger there.

"Oh, yeah. It can be a reward for good behavior."

Justin snorted, eyes rolling.

"Brat." He pinched Justin's right nipple.

"Hey! You bruised it already!"

"Bet the ache is really good now."

"Still, leave it alone. It's all... dark."

"So?" Chris thought it looked amazing, all swollen and bruised. In fact he'd like to see it more swollen.

"So? Did you have a stroke while we were apart, old man?" Oh, someone was feeling up to teasing.

"I'll show you old." He growled and rolled back on top of Justin, mouth landing hard on Justin's.

This time Justin opened for him, laughing into the kiss. He traced Justin's teeth, his gums, memorizing the shape of his lover's mouth. God, he was stupid for this man. Had been for years. He rolled his hips easily, their cocks rubbing together, Justin's hands trapped in their cuffs between their bellies.

"Take off the cuffs. It's weird."

"No. You flipped me off. They can stay on for awhile."

"No?" Justin looked utterly shocked.

"That's right."

"But... you're not my coach, Coach."

"You can keep calling me Coach. It works. Or you can call me sir or master." He thought coach worked well for them.

"Master?" Justin looked totally stunned. "When did you get all... leather and weird?"

"I've always been leather and weird, Justin." He'd never shared that part of his life with Justin when he'd been Justin's coach. Much as he would have liked to; it wouldn't have been right.

"So you just... did it with other guys?"

"More read about it and joined an online club so I could learn to do it properly."

"A club?"

"Yep. It's for people who are into BDSM. They recommended Silver Linings to me—it's the best club in the city. I can take you if you want to see."

"No. I don't... I. No! I'm not..."

Oh, Justin so was. He just didn't know it yet.

"Well, it's not going anywhere." He gave Justin a slow smile.

"No. I'm not either."

Somehow he didn't think Justin meant it like he did.

"No, you're not," he said quietly.

Justin sighed, the sound so lost.

"You're not going anywhere at all—you're staying right here with me."

"I have to go back to work, pay bills. Stuff."

"You're working for me now." He needed a coaching assistant. He'd told Justin that last night and he hadn't been kidding.

"What?"

"I need a coaching assistant, and you need a job that feeds your soul instead of sucking it out."

"I have a job. I use my degree." Justin hated that job. If he was getting anything but a paycheck out of it, Chris would eat his shorts.

"Tell me you'd rather do that than assistant coach swimmers with me. Look me in the eye and tell me that."

Justin met his eyes. "I..."

"You can't do it, can you? You'd love to work with me, work with the kids, find the ones with that spark, the potential." It would be like magic to have Justin by his side twenty-four seven again. Only better because they had this now.

"No. No, I want to be eighteen again."

"Don't we all?" He kissed Justin's nose. "Trust me, you can have a lot more fun now than you could then."

"I just... Nothing's right anymore. Nothing. They don't tell you that you win and then life is just... nothing."

"Then we'll make it something. Maybe I made the wrong decision in forcing you to go out and make your own way for awhile, but I'm ready to fix that. Are you? You're going to be so happy with me, Just. You have to at least give it a chance."

"Maybe." Justin sighed softly. "Take the cuffs off me. I don't want to play games. I want a shower and something to drink."

"I'm taking them off, but not because this was a game, but because you didn't know the rules." He met Justin's eyes. "I am not giving up on you."

"Maybe you have to."

"No fucking way."

Justin held his hands up. "Please."

He took hold of Justin's hands. "Are you going to give us a chance?"

"I don't know. I don't know what to think. We're naked. Together. In a bed."

"And it's great. You're loving it, if you admit it."

"I've never been totally naked in bed with someone before."

That nearly broke his heart. Except for the part of him that was glad he would be so many firsts for Justin. "Now you have."

"Yeah." Justin didn't mention the cuffs again.

"You've got a fantastic body, too. It deserves to be naked in bed with me."

That made Justin chuckle. "You still have a weird sense of humor."

"There's nothing wrong with my sense of humor, nothing at all."

"Weird. Weird. Weird."

He stuck his tongue out at Justin. Justin tried to reach up, grab him, but those sweet wrists were still bound. He chuckled and touched Justin's belly button. Justin's abs rolled, rocked, jerked under his touch.

"Sexy boy." He whispered the words, stroked the beautiful muscles.

"I... That..." Justin's hips rolled up, moving that cock toward his hand.

"Feels good?" he suggested, skirting Justin's needy prick.

"Uh-huh. It's very good."

He smiled, fingers circling Justin's hip.

"I missed your massages." Justin stretched for him.

"Is that all you missed?"

"No."

"No?" He'd bet Justin missed the rules.

Justin shook his head. "I missed midnight pancakes. I missed watching TV in hotel rooms. I missed my best friend."

"I'm sorry. I should have called you a long time ago. I made the assumption that if you didn't call me, you didn't want me back in your life."

Justin chuckled. "I don't know, Coach. You were pretty clear that you were ready to move on."

Is that how it had felt to Justin?

He shook his head. "I was trying to be clear that you were free to find your own way, to not have me to answer to constantly. I was all you knew, if I'd kept you once you retired, that wouldn't have been fair to you." He'd been telling Justin what to do since he was twelve years old, it wouldn't have been right to move that into the bedroom without Justin having a chance to see what was out there, what he could do with the world and make his own decisions.

Letting Justin go had been the hardest thing Chris had ever done.

"I didn't want to be kept. I just... I lost my whole world, man. My career, my home, my best friend. I went home for a couple of months, but... everyone was like— we sacrificed for you, we're done, get out."

"I didn't know, Just. I'm sorry. That was not my intention. I wanted you, but not because I was all you knew."

"Well, I'm not worth anything now. I make twenty six thousand a year at an entry level job, I share an apartment with a guy, and I drink a lot."

Chris growled. "You're worth a hell of a lot to me, Justin. And I will start reinforcing the no putting yourself down rule the next time you do it."

"Or what? You're going to make me less useful?"

"Or there will be a punishment." He growled and

slapped Justin's ass, twice. "That was for putting yourself down. Again."

"You spanked me!"

"I did. You keep putting yourself down and it'll happen again."

"You can't spank me, man."

"I just did. And I'll do it again if I have to. We'll work on a system or rules and punishments and rewards."

Justin looked at him, lips opening, then closing, then opening again. He leaned in and pushed their mouths together, tongue sliding into Justin's lips. Justin leaned up, right into the kiss, tasting him. He cupped the back of Justin's head, supporting his lover as the kiss deepened. When Justin moaned for him, fingers grabbing at him, he wanted to crow.

His free hand slid around to grab at Justin's ass, pulling them together so their pricks rubbed. Justin wasn't hard, but he was getting there, beginning to respond to him. His own prick was hard, sliding against that lovely belly. Their kisses went on and on, Justin diving into them now, hungry for him. He drew Justin's hands up over his head and rolled them so he was on top of the strong body.

"Coach." Justin's eyes were wide.

"Right here, Just. Gonna love on you."

Those big eyes searched his, sparkling and bright. "I always wanted you to love me. I thought you did."

"I did. I *do*," he insisted.

"I don't know what to do."

"I do. So all you have to do is listen to me."

Justin actually relaxed. "I'm good at that."

"You are. You've always been good at that." He licked Justin's cheek.

Justin nodded, chuckled. God, his boy was beautiful. He took another kiss and reached down to jack Justin's prick. Almost fully hard now, the sweet cock fit in his palm. Humming, he jacked it, working that pretty prick. It didn't take long for Justin to begin rolling toward him.

"That's it, sweet J."

Justin moaned softly, hips driving into his touch.

"I want you, J. I want to be inside you." He was fiercely glad he would be the first one.

"Does it hurt?"

"No, it doesn't." Not when you prepped and cared and took your time.

"Okay." Justin hid in the curve of his shoulder.

"My brave boy," he murmured, thumb teasing at Justin's slit.

"I just want to feel things again. To be awake."

"I'll make sure you're awake, J. Every fucking day of the week."

"I..." Justin groaned and pushed up, taking his mouth in a needy kiss.

He pushed his finger into Justin's slit again, then began to stroke quickly.

"Oh. Oh." Justin's eyes rolled. "Oh, do that again."

"This?" He stroked only, teasing his boy.

Justin shook his head, so serious. "No. No, the other."

Smiling, he dug his thumb into that sweet little slit again. Justin groaned, abs going taut.

"You're allowed to come," he murmured.

"Allowed..." Justin bucked for him.

"That's right. Let go and come for me. Do it now." He pressed in again, and Justin moaned, seed covering his thumb.

Groaning, he took Justin's mouth, wordlessly telling Justin how great that was. His good babe.

He found the lube on his bedside table and worked it open, got his fingers good and slippery while they kissed. Justin's eyelids were heavy, lips parted.

"You ready, J? Ready to feel me inside you?" He slipped his fingers along Justin's crack.

"I don't know." That was honest.

"Then let's see." He teased his fingers against Justin's hole.

Justin tensed, then relaxed. Eased. Let him in.

"Good boy." He wriggled the tip of his finger inside Justin's body.

"That feels weird."

"Good weird." It wasn't a question, and he pushed the finger deeper.

Justin's toes curled, legs moving restlessly. He pressed in even father, searching for Justin's gland.

"You're touching me inside."

"I am." His finger slid over the smooth little bump of Justin's gland.

Justin went stiff, still, eyes huge. He just smiled and did it again.

"I. I. Coach?"

"It's good, isn't it?" He nudged Justin's gland a couple more times, knowing the sensation had to be shooting up Justin's spine.

"Uh-huh." Justin's eyes crossed.

It made him grin and he did it again, loving that he could make this good for Justin.

"Coach." Justin tugged at the cuffs, gasped.

He slid another finger inside his boy. Justin gasped, hole fluttering around his fingers. He pushed them in and out, working to find Justin's gland with every push in, to keep the sensations hot and bright. His boy was slick and needy, beginning to move into his touch.

Groaning, he pressed kiss after kiss on Justin's mouth as he worked the sweet channel around his fingers. Justin was moaning, crying out into his mouth, over and over. He worked a third finger in with the first two, spreading

Justin wider. Getting his boy ready for his cock.

"Oh. Oh, that aches."

He slid his fingers out and added more lube, then pushed them back in again, slowly finger-fucking Justin. "Getting you ready for my prick, J."

"Oh, god." Justin arched, body rippling.

"Gonna make you feel so good."

"Please." Justin was so hungry for touch.

"You want to go hands and knees or face to face?" Hands and knees would be easier, but there was a better connection when they were face to face.

"I want to know it's you."

"It's me, Justin. No one has ever done this with you and no one ever will." He let his fingers slide away. "Lie on your back, and grab your knees for me."

Justin leaned back, pulled his knees up and back, exposing himself.

"Oh, damn. J." Groaning, he moved between Justin's legs, his hands dragging along Justin's inner thighs.

"I'm aching."

"I'm going to make it better, I promise."

"Okay." The words of trust meant so much.

He slipped his fingers back into Justin's body, fucking him gently.

"Oh." Justin's face went slack.

God, he could live for this. He spread his fingers wide apart.

"I... That." Justin reached for him with his cuffed hands.

He kissed Justin's palm.

"Oh..." Justin moaned, breath hitching.

Smiling, he let his fingers slide from Justin's body so he could grab a condom. He smoothed it over his prick, slicked himself, touch careful. He didn't want to be close. He wanted this to last and last. He wanted to blow

Justin's mind and show him just how good it was. He settled between Justin's legs and grabbed them, putting them over his shoulders and exposing that sweet little hole.

Justin blushed dark, eyes squeezing shut.

He stroked one cheek. "Look at me, J. That's why we did it like this, remember?"

"Right." Justin swallowed hard. "It's big."

"I know. It'll be good, though. I promise."

"You promise." Justin moaned, eyes glittering.

"I promise, babe."

He hefted Justin's legs higher over his shoulders and pressed the tip of his cock against Justin's hole. Justin pulled in a deep, deep breath, lips parted, eyes on him. He held that blue gaze as he slowly pushed into the tight heat. That tight, tiny hole fought him, scraping along his cock as he thrust.

"Breathe, Just." He was holding his own breath, Justin just so damn tight.

"Trying." Justin could hold his breath, so long.

He reached up and pinched one of Justin's nipples. Justin gasped, sucked in a deep breath.

"Better." He started moving faster. He slowly filled his boy, inch by inch, popping the sweet cherry. "Fucking perfect, Just."

"I. So full." Justin moaned, a dull flush climbing up his belly.

"Keep breathing. It'll ease in a moment."

"'kay." Justin sucked in another breath, moaned.

Chris kept moving slowly, letting Justin get used to the feeling. Letting his hand drag down along Justin's belly, he pet his lover, soothed Justin's nerves. He could fucking touch Justin forever and a week, just to make up for lost time.

The death grip around his cock eased, let him breathe, move.

"Nice, babe." He slid carefully, slowly, working his prick in and out of Justin's amazing heat.

"I. You're... Oh, fuck."

"Uh-huh." He wanted Justin incoherent and out of his mind with pleasure.

"But..." Justin cried out, hands twisting in the cuffs as he pushed in, dragged his cock over his boy's gland. He pushed his prick across that spot again, moving slowly but deliberately, watching Justin the whole time. Justin's body jerked, shoulders leaving the bed, cock going dark.

"Good, isn't it?" He moved over Justin's gland again.

"Uhn." He thought that was a yes.

It was killing him, but he kept moving slowly, kept working that little bit of flesh as he did. Justin pushed his cuffed hands between them, fingers wrapping around his cock, pulling hard.

"No." The word growled out of him, and Chris grabbed the cuffs, returning Justin's hands back up over Justin's head. "No touching 'til I say so."

"Coach! Coach, I need!"

"Let it build, J. We're going to take our time—this isn't a race."

"Everything's a race. Please."

"Not this." He pressed his hand on Justin's, not enough to hurt, but enough that Justin couldn't ignore the pressure, knew exactly who was in charge.

"No fair." How many times had Justin said that to him? The familiar words made him smile.

"This is love, Just. All's fair in love and swimming."

"You don't... Oh. Oh, Coach..." Justin's body jerked around him.

"Wait for my order, Justin."

"Coach..." Justin moaned, twisting underneath him.

"I know you can wait." He knew Justin wanted to obey him. Justin nodded, lips parted, slick. "Good boy."

He loved how Justin's cheeks went dark at his words.

He punched in a few more times before wrapping his hand around Justin's prick. Justin whined softly, fingers curling. His hand moved in long, slow pulls.

"Coach. Coach. Coach." The word came in time with his strokes.

"Okay, Justin. You can come now."

Justin's eyes went wide and he could feel Justin's body, rippling around him.

"That's it, Just. Give it to me." He pushed in hard, prick rubbing past Justin's gland, the scent of come sudden and perfect.

Fuck, yes. He let his head hang down, hips slamming in. It was so fucking good. Justin was tight, his body rippling with his orgasm and Chris was pretty sure he'd died and gone to heaven. If he hadn't, he could just stay right here.

He kept moving, tiny little motions that sent shivers down his spine. Justin moaned for him, the sound whisper soft.

"Shit, Just. I knew it would be good, but this... fuck."

Justin nodded, exhaled softly. He pressed soft kisses on Justin's face.

"Worth waiting for?" he asked.

Justin nodded, once.

"I'm glad you waited, too. I want to be the one to pop all your cherries."

"I don't think I have any left." Sweet, innocent boy.

Chris just chuckled.

"I... You hungry?"

"I could eat. You offering to make me breakfast?"

Justin snorted. "You're funny. I make coffee and Eggo waffles. I was offering to buy you a bagel."

"Damn, I was hoping you'd learned some culinary skills in the last few years." Neither of them had ever been good in the kitchen. Not in all the years he'd coached Justin.

"Right. Eggos. Ham sandwiches. Ramen noodles. Frozen pizzas. We're bachelors."

"Not anymore. We're a couple now. I'm thinking cooking lessons..."

It could be a part of Justin's duties. Justin needed a schedule, he always had. Being in charge of meals would make a great anchor.

"I don't cook." Justin rubbed his forehead. "Man, I need an aspirin."

"I'm not surprised—no more drinking." He got up and padded to the bathroom, coming back with a glass of water and a bottle of Tylenol.

"Not until after breakfast, for sure."

"Not without permission, anytime of the day." They were going to have a long list of rules, he was sure.

"What? I'm legal."

"That's not the point, J. It's going to be one of the rules. Besides, you won't need to get drunk anymore."

Justin took the pain pill, then grabbed his shorts. "Bagels?"

"Sure. Sounds good. I mean it about cooking classes, though." Chris pulled on a t-shirt and a pair of shorts before grabbing one of his shirts to give to Justin. "That should fit you."

"Thanks. I'll wash it and get it back to you."

"You'll be here so there's no 'getting it back to me' needed."

"I have to go home. I have work."

"I'll come and help you pack up. We can share my office." He knew damn well Justin could create webpages anywhere, as long as he had his computer.

"I have to think about this. I have to give notice. I have to think."

"You can work out your notice from here." He went to Justin and wrapped his hand around Justin's cheeks, tilted Justin's face so they were looking into each other's eyes. "Tell me you don't want to be with me."

"I... I have to go home, Coach. Think."

"Thinking was never your strong point, Just."

Justin's eyes went wide, the look suddenly hurt. "No. No, it wasn't. I really have to run, man. I'll see you." Then Justin left him, standing there.

"Justin! Wait." He sighed. He hadn't meant to hurt Justin's feelings.

He grabbed his wallet and put it in his back pocket, going after his boy. He had to remember that things were different now, that Justin wasn't his swimmer. His boy, yes, but not his swimmer. Besides, Justin wasn't quite with the program yet. The boy wanted to be, would be.

Chris was betting his heart on it.

Chapter Four

Justin jogged toward home, only starting to sweat about two miles into it, his bare feet hitting the sand. God. God, what was wrong with him?

A car horn honked. He ignored it. He wasn't on the road, wasn't in anyone's way. Another honk followed the first, then a third time. He turned to look, jogging in place. Oh. Coach. Damn.

He waved, pulled the t-shirt out of his pocket and headed over. "Here's your shirt. I didn't sweat in it."

"Justin. I don't care if you sweat on my t-shirt." Coach jerked his head toward the passenger side. "Get in."

"I... I'm just heading home, you know? Working out."

"Get in the car, Just. Please."

"I'm not stupid." It hadn't been exactly what he'd meant to say, but it was what he'd been thinking, the whole way. He slid into the passenger's seat.

"I know. And I'm sorry I said what I did. I didn't mean it the way you took it, but I shouldn't have said it."

"I mean, I'm really, really not." He stared at his hands. "I know that I'm not... I got my degree, I have a job, an apartment. I'm not dumb. I just miss being who I was."

"I know, J. I didn't mean that I thought you were dumb. It was more... that you over think things and work yourself into knots with it."

"Yeah. I guess. Can you drop me off at home, please?"

"Can I come in and help you pack?"

Justin shook his head. "Coach, you don't need me."
He knew this. He didn't need himself.

"That's not in the least bit true. I do need you." Coach
started the car.

"You have swimmers."

"I don't have the man I love." Chris spoke softly, but
very clearly.

"You used to love."

"That I love. I've been pining for you, Justin."

"You made me call you."

"Of course I made you call me. I ran your life. I didn't
think it would be right for me to turn around and tell you
that you were staying with me as my lover now that the
swimming was over."

"And now you just want me? No. We have to date. We
have to see if we are compatible and stuff."

"See if we're compatible? We were together for
years—you know we're compatible. But if you want to
be wooed, I can woo you."

They pulled up in front of his apartment building and
they sat there.

Chris finally broke the silence. "There's no 'just' about
any of this, you know. Besides you."

"Can we go out tonight? Like normal people? My
treat?"

"We are normal people, but yes, we can go out your
treat. Where are you taking me?"

"Vinny's? You like their garlic bread a lot." He
remembered that.

"I do. Now I think you're trying to fatten me up."
Coach winked at him.

"You look great, Coach. Honest."

Coach chuckled. "I was only teasing, but that's still
good to hear."

His stomach growled, loud enough to hear. He really needed that bagel.

Chris touched it briefly, making it flare with heat. "Let me take you to breakfast before I drop you off at home."

"I'll sweat on your shirt."

Coach looked at him like he'd lost his mind. "Is it made of gold?"

"Your shirt? I don't think so." And he'd seen gold before.

"Then what's the problem with you sweating on it?" Coach turned the car into a little strip mall near his place that had a deli in it.

"I was trying to be polite, man."

"You don't need to be polite with me, Justin. We know each other too well."

"Still, that's part of dating. Not sweating on a guy's clothes." He managed, barely, not to grin.

"Even if we get all hot and bothered? 'Cause it seems to me like sweating on a guy's clothes could very much be a part of dating." Coach parked and slipped the keys out of the ignition, turning to him.

He couldn't fight the smile this time, pulling the shirt on to hide his chuckles.

Coach came around and opened his door for him. "Just like a proper date, right?"

"Dork." He was feeling a little more like he could breathe, though. "Cinnamon sugar bagel or chocolate chip?"

"You know the answer to that, Just." Coach had a sweet tooth he liked to deny, but anything with sugar was going to get devoured.

"I do." He headed in, ordered three cinnamon sugar and one raisin bagel, two coffees, and two huge orange juices.

"We're definitely going to have to work out after a

breakfast like this." Coach looked happy with his choices, though, handing money to the lady behind the cash.

"I've already worked out, Coach." He grabbed the tray and they moved to one of the little tables for two.

"Right. Running away."

"Don't be an ass."

"You were." Coach reached across the table and squeezed his hand.

"Just running. Not running away."

One of Coach's eyebrows went up, but he didn't say anything. And when he bit into his bagel, he closed his eyes. "Still warm."

Justin grabbed one half of the raisin, spreading cream cheese and devouring it.

"I forgot how much I love watching you eat."

Justin felt his cheeks heat. "Thank you." Okay, that made him a little goofy. It also made him self-conscious as he ate, noticing that Coach *was* watching him. He started fidgeting, unnerved.

"What's wrong?"

"You're watching me."

"Sorry." Coach grinned and grabbed another cinnamon and sugar bagel.

"Uh-huh." Coach was lying. There wasn't an ounce of sorry there.

Leaning in, Coach reached out and slid a finger on the corner of his lips. "Cream cheese."

"Thank you." He licked his lips.

Coach made a soft sound, eyes on his mouth. His tongue flicked out again, the action instinctive. This time Coach's sound was louder, a sweet groan. He buried his face in his orange juice, heart racing.

"You know much I wanted to express my feelings before? How hard it was watching you do things like that?"

"No." No, he didn't know, but he wanted to.

"It was fucking hard, Just. It's amazing, being able to watch, being able to let out how I'm feeling."

The words felt so good, like a balm or something. So did Coach's gaze. It was like a touch.

"How's your bagel?" he asked.

"Sweet." Coach smiled at him.

"Just like you like them."

"Yeah. We know each other pretty well."

He nodded. They'd spent a lot of time together, in each other's pockets.

Coach's foot touched his under the table. Justin caught himself grinning like the world's biggest idiot. Of course Coach was grinning back at him, just as wide.

"Drink your juice." This was stupid. Fun. New. Exciting. But stupid.

"You drink your juice," Coach countered.

He had. "I'm drinking my coffee."

"Brat."

Justin grinned, then dutifully sipped his juice. Coach's smile was cocky, the man's feet playing with his before one slid up his calf.

"You can't play footsie over bagels. It's a law."

"Then I'm breaking the law. In my defense, I've never heard of this law before."

"It's well-known," he insisted.

"In what circles?" Coach was still rubbing his leg with a foot.

His cock was starting to fill, swell. Circles. Circles? What the hell was Coach talking about again?

"Well?" Coach asked softly, feet not letting up for an instant.

"Well, what?" His eyes crossed.

Coach smiled at him, looking pleased with himself.

"What are you grinning about?" Justin had lost the

thread somewhere... about the time that foot began playing with his.

"You've forgotten what we were talking about."

"I just... was thinking about something else."

"And what's that?" Coach's grin got bigger, if that was possible.

"Bagels," he lied.

The snort he got told him exactly what Coach thought of that. Justin winked over, feeling real for the first time in days. Months. Laughing, Coach slid his foot up between Justin's legs. Maybe things were going to be okay, a little.

Coach's gaze never left him, a warmth in his eyes. Justin smiled, leaned back in his chair. Better. This was better. Coach's foot slid between his upper thighs.

"Coach, be good."

"Oh, I think I'm being very good."

He shook his head. "You're not."

"You're not enjoying this?" Coach's toes nudged his package.

"I... Hey!"

Coach gave him this 'innocent' look.

"Stop it. You're not innocent."

Coach started to laugh. That foot stayed where it was, though. He scooted back, getting himself out of range.

"Tshaw. You were enjoying that." Coach was practically pouting at him.

"We're in a bagel shop."

"It's not that busy," countered Coach.

Justin snorted. "That's not the point."

"No? Then what is, Just?"

He rolled his eyes. "You can't do that."

"What? A little under the table where no one can see it footsie?"

"Yes!"

Dork.

Coach shook his head. "But I *am* doing it."

"Nope. I moved."

"All right, let me rephrase, I *was* doing it. I don't remember you being so semantic."

"I got smarter." And more bored.

"And sexier."

"I don't know about that." It sure felt good to hear it, though.

"Trust me. You are." The heat in Coach's eyes was almost as arousing as that foot on his package had been.

"Finish your bagel."

"We bringing the extra ones home?" Coach took a bite.

"I thought... Weren't we going out tonight?"

"Sure. We can't bring the bagels home if we're having supper out?"

"I thought I was going to my home and you were going to yours."

"You want to stick with that plan, do you?"

"No, I really want to go somewhere and watch a movie and just rest. I'm tired." He blinked. "I mean..." Jesus, he had diarrhea of the fucking mouth.

"That can be arranged. You want to come back to my place or hit a theater?"

"I..." He hated theaters; Coach knew that.

"So, you'll come home and we'll eat popcorn and watch movies and snuggle under a blanket on my couch."

"Okay. Okay, I'd like that." It sounded like heaven, actually.

"Then let's take these two bagels home. We can have them when we're tired of popcorn."

He found himself tucked into Coach's side again, in the car, before he knew it. Much as he'd wanted to go home and think, he couldn't think of anywhere he'd rather be.

They watched all four *Die Hard* movies amid much popcorn and sweet bagel leftovers and Justin dozing in Chris' arms. They'd sat and watched a lot of movies together over the years, but he'd never been able to hold Justin like this, like the man was his.

"Should I call for pizza before we start on something else?" he suggested when it started getting dark.

"You don't mind staying in?"

Like he'd bitch about this. Ever. "Not for a second. Anchovies and olives and extra cheese, right?" Justin was a freak when it came to pizza. He'd learned to live with it.

"Uh-huh." Justin grinned. "Sacky's Pizza calls that the Justin Special. It's on the menu."

"Christ, I take it you order a lot more pizza now than you used to be allowed to eat when you were training." He grabbed the phone and looked up Sacky's on his laptop.

"Uh-huh. Five, six times a week."

He stared at Justin. "Seriously?" Oh, he was so getting cooking lessons for Justin and making that part of Justin's duties.

"Uh-huh." Justin shrugged. "My roomie pays for half."

"What's he going to do now that you're moving in with me?" He wasn't taking no for an answer on that point.

"I..." Justin shook his head. "You're stubborn."

"Yep. I am." He found the phone number for the pizza place Justin liked and called them up. "Large Justin Special, please." He gave them his address and added a couple slices of apple pie to the order.

When he was done, Justin spoke. "I don't know if we're going to talk about moving in together..."

"Why wouldn't we talk about it?"

"Because I don't know if I can. I have responsibilities."

"Your job. I've already told you that you can share my office with me for work." He would have an answer to every single one of Justin's objections. He was serious about this.

"I work in the office, not at home. They don't trust people."

Chris frowned. "Then hand in your notice. You don't want to work for someone who doesn't trust you."

"I can't just quit my job!"

"Why not?" He had a job for Justin. A legitimate job that included things that Justin loved.

"Because I'm a grownup and the economy sucks and stuff?"

"But you have a job to move on to. That's a very grown up thing—moving from a job you hate to a job you love."

Justin met his eyes, chewing on his bottom lip, worrying it. "I don't know. I don't want to see you fall in love with another swimmer."

"Justin." He moved to the couch and straddled his boy, cupped Justin's face. "I'm in love with you. If *we* find another swimmer to take all the way, it'll be something you and I share."

"I don't know..." God, had Just always stressed everything?

"Just. Are you happy where you are?"

"No." That was sure.

"Then why are you having a problem accepting my job offer?"

"Because I don't know if I want to watch people swim all day."

"That's not all the job entails. You'd keep stats, make notes, watch the competition, get in the water and demonstrate strokes. Hell, you can swim races with the kids—let them feel what competition is really like."

There was still the small matter of Justin not liking his

current job at all. Chris didn't think it was better than watching swimmers at all.

Justin sighed again, focus turning to the TV. "I'll think about it."

"Besides, you can still live with me and work at the evil day job." He just wanted Justin with him. The rest really was just details. Sure they had to deal with them, but together they could.

"Come sit down, Coach."

He sat back down, pulling Justin into him. "I want you here with me, Justin."

Justin's answer was a soft, quiet sigh.

"I want so much for us."

"I try not to want stuff. Is that weird?"

"More sad than weird, I think. Your life isn't over, Just. Not by a long shot."

Justin wouldn't look at him. "Feels like it, a little."

"I will spend the rest of my days making sure you feel special and loved and important." He would not let Justin feel like he was a has-been, or unimportant or less than anything.

"What if I don't deserve it anymore?"

He snorted. "That's a bunch of horseshit and you know it."

"I don't. Maybe I used up all the important shit and now it's just beige."

"Move in with me, Just, and I'll show you just how un-beige life can be."

"You're pushy." Justin's words were warm, fond.

"That's nothing new." He made his living being pushy.

"Nope."

He pulled Justin in close. "You never said what movies you wanted to move on to."

"*X-Men*?" Justin cuddled, relaxing against him.

"Cool, we've got all of those." He pressed a kiss on

top of Justin's head and went over to find the movies.

"You've got all of them."

"Yep." He knew they were some of Justin's favorites and eventually Justin would see his stuff as theirs.

"Cool." Justin was curled in the huge, fluffy blanket, feet tucked up under him.

He wanted the man here with him now. For good. He wanted Justin's smile, the husky chuckles. He wanted that sweet body next to him, under him. He wanted Justin.

Chris put the first movie into the Blu-Ray and went back to sit with his boy. Justin moved closer, immediately, snuggling right in. How could his boy have any hesitation about moving in? They fit together perfectly.

Justin's fingers stroked his belly, moving lazily. He hummed, tugged Justin a little closer and if he was more focused on Justin than the movie, well he'd seen it before, hadn't he?

Justin was almost asleep when the pizza came. Chris slid out from the couch and went to pay for the pizza. He handed over the money and headed back to the living room, admiring his boy on the sofa.

"You look like you belong, Just." He set the pizza on the table along with the cans of pop and pie he'd ordered.

"Thanks. It smells good." Justin sat up, smiled over at him.

He shook his head, but smiled back. It was a crazy-assed combination and he'd missed ordering it over the last four years. Why had he waited so long for Justin to call? Oh, right, he'd had some crazy idea about being noble and shit.

There were tissues on the side-table, so they didn't need plates and he opened the box as he sat back down next to Justin. They fell on the pizza, noshing and laughing about the movie, side by side. It was like old times, but with the added benefit of love and sex being in the mix.

When they were done eating, he grabbed Justin's hand and sucking the grease off one particularly messy finger.

"Coach!" Justin sounded partly outraged, party turned on.

He let an eyebrow go up and took the finger in deep, letting his teeth scrape along it. Justin's lips parted. Humming, he bobbed his head, sucking Justin's finger like it was his boy's cock.'

"Oh, damn..." Justin wiggled, eyes focused.

He came off the finger really slowly, gaze on Justin's.

"I..." Justin groaned. "The pizza's good."

"Just the pizza?"

"You're not good. You're wicked."

He chuckled and sucked in one of Justin's other fingers.

"S...see? Wicked?"

He bit at Justin's fingertip. Justin pulled away, hid his hands.

"You can't hide from me, Just." He took Justin's hand, held it.

"I can." Justin's breath quickened.

"No. I see you." He took Justin's hand and bit one finger after another.

"N...no. No biting." Look at his boy blush.

"You like the biting."

Justin loved the biting. He bit Justin's thumb.

"No..." Justin gasped for him, fingers curling.

He licked Justin's thumb, from where he'd bitten, all the way down to the pad. Which he bit. That tiny, hungry little sound Justin made was perfect—breathless, needy. It made him groan as he sucked on Justin's hand.

"More. Oh, fuck." Justin's throat was working.

He moved down to bite at the inside of Justin's wrist. Justin's fingers curled, a soft moan on the air. He licked away the little stings left by his teeth, and then bit again.

"You're making me hard."

"Good." It was the point, after all. That and making Justin feel amazing.

Justin pushed closer, shoving the pizza box out of the way. "No more biting."

Right, because Justin was just *hating* the biting, and it was totally turning his boy off. He snorted and bit at the skin on the inside of Justin's elbow, letting his teeth scrape. That made Justin chuckle, stretch a little. He licked circles around the spot, tongue pressing hard enough not to tickle.

Justin pushed forward, body snuggling into his. "Enough."

"No, I don't think so." He could feel Justin's prick, pushing against his thigh, and he rubbed his own growing length against his boy.

"Uh-huh. Have to."

"Have to what?" He drew Justin's arm up and nibbled his way to Justin's underarm.

"S... I... Oh, fuck..."

He tugged on Justin's underarm hair with his teeth, then moved to lap at one of Justin's nipples.

"Oh. Oh, careful."

He smiled, just before he bit that nipple.

"Ow!" Justin jerked, arched up into his mouth.

Chris wrapped his lips around the sweet flesh and began to suck, soothing the bite and marking the nipple at the same time. He wanted these sweet titties swollen and rosy, sensitive and aching. All the time. He wanted to be able to just blow on them and have Justin's prick pay attention. He wanted Justin begging for him to bruise them. He wanted Justin plugged and bound and needing. He wanted Justin needing so badly it ached. Hell, he wanted everything.

He let go of Justin's arm to play with his left nipple, fingers pinching and tugging as he kept working on the right with his mouth.

"They ache. They ache, Coach. You'll make them bruised."

"Yes." Justin was catching on. He switched nipples, sucking on the left and pinching the right.

Fingers wrapped around his wrist, squeezing him. Holding on. He bit the tip of Justin's nipple as he twisted the other one making Justin cry out. Justin twisted, groaning his name, needing him. He tugged at Justin's sweats, pulling them down. His boy was hard, prick red and wet-tipped, begging for abuse.

"Needy boy."

How had Justin gone so long with only the occasional hand job?

"Uh-huh. I want."

"I can see that." He moved in, and took just the head of Justin's cock into his mouth.

The lean body went still for a heartbeat, then Justin humped up into his lips. He pulled back. His boy wasn't getting off just yet.

"Coach..." Wanting, hungry—this was the perfect mindset to play with.

"Yeah, Just?" He licked at the base of Justin's prick.

"I... You make me ache."

"Good." He'd keep saying it until Justin realized that was why he did it, and that it was good.

"Aching isn't good, is it?" Justin asked.

"Aching is very good," he insisted.

Justin shook his head, chuckled.

"It is. You'll see." He gave Justin his best wicked smile and rolled the man's lovely balls. One of Justin's legs drew up, exposing the man's sweet, swollen hole. Someone was into it big time.

He leaned in, nuzzled Justin's abs, the flat belly. His fingers pressed against Justin's inner thigh, spreading that leg wider. Justin spread for him, the sight making his mouth dry. He pressed a finger against that sweet hole. Justin offered him a full body shiver.

He put his finger at Justin's mouth. "Suck, babe."

Justin didn't hesitate at all, lips wrapping around his finger, the suction fierce and sharp.

"Fuck." His hips jerked. His boy sucked harder, tongue sliding on his fingertip. He wanted to feel that amazing suction around his prick. "Want you to suck me."

Justin nodded, moaning low. Chris climbed onto the couch, opening his jeans. When Justin tried to sit up, he shook his head, moving to straddle Justin's chest. He wanted to fuck his boy's mouth.

"Like that." He rubbed the tip of his prick against those pretty lips.

Justin opened up for him, eyes closing. He slipped the tip of his cock into Justin's mouth. Justin started sucking, pulling hard and steady at his cock.

"Oh, fuck." It felt so good—Justin's mouth was made for sucking.

He watched as he pushed in, then pulled away, his prick slick and shiny. Justin was made to suck, mouth eager and hot, hungry. Chris grabbed the arm of the couch, using it for leverage as he started rocking, pushing his cock a little deeper into Justin's mouth with each thrust. He was careful not to choke, to give Justin more than was easy, not too much.

His eager boy was giving him amazing suction, making him moan with it. He loved this beautiful son of a bitch. He moved faster, prick sliding on Justin's tongue. Justin moaned around him, sucking harder. The vibrations from Justin's moan made him shiver and he started moving faster.

He was going to come and then they could play. Start those steps toward submission.

"Keep sucking, J. You're made for it." Made for him. His words made Justin swallow, moan for him.

"Soon." He didn't want to go off yet, but he was going to, very soon.

Justin groaned, tongue slapping his cock.

"Fuck!" He jerked, pushing in deeper.

Justin's eyes flew open, those bright blue eyes staring him down. He held that gaze, pulling back out then pushing in again. Justin swallowed convulsively.

"Oh, God." He jerked, his balls pulling up tight against his body as he came down Justin's throat.

Justin grabbed for him, holding his thighs with sweaty palms.

"Love you." He growled out the words, stroking Justin's cheeks as his boy swallowed around his cock.

He thought there were tears in Justin's eyes.

He pulled out, fingers stroking over Justin's lips. "Just?"

"Uh-huh?"

"You okay?"

"Uh-huh." Justin nodded. "Just, I... it's you."

"I'm right here. I'm not going anywhere." He reached down, touched those swollen, parted lips, and Justin kissed the tip of his finger.

"Mmm. You're something special Justin Pattern."

"I was."

"No, Justin," he insisted. "You *are*, you fucking are."

Justin wanted to believe him, he could tell.

"My Justin. Gonna show you how special." Even if he had to spend all his life doing it.

Chapter Five

Justin rolled his head on his shoulders, sighing as his boss kept yelling at them about something he didn't give a shit about. No one was listening, no one ever did, and his shift was over in eight minutes and he was going to just... Sit here until the asshole wound down, but he liked to pretend he was going to storm off.

His cell went off, buzzing insistently in his pocket. He ignored it, at least until the third time, then he stood. "Emergency." He was off the clock, damn it. He looked at the call display. It was Coach. He slid out of the room.

"Hey, Coach. What's up?"

"Hey, Justin. I came to pick you up."

"You did?" He blushed, grinned, unaccountably pleased.

"Yeah. I'm parked across the street. Are you ready to come home or should I go find a coffee somewhere?"

"I'm ready." He was possibly in trouble.

"Cool. Come on down. I was thinking we could go out for supper. Man cannot live on pizza alone."

"Sure he can. I'll be..."

"Justin! What the hell were you doing? Walking out of a meeting?" Rob was coming for him, voice strident. "You want to keep your job, you moron?"

Justin heard Coach growl through the line. "I can come up there, Just."

"Jesus Christ, you're replaceable. Is that what you want? I have monkeys more capable than you!" Rob went on.

Justin sighed. Really?

Coach had clearly heard, his voice angry in Justin's ear. "Justin, tell that little pissant to go to hell. I have a job for you. One where you'll be appreciated."

"I have to go." He wasn't sure which man he was talking to, but he knew that he was heading outside to Coach.

"Don't you dare walk out on me!" Rob was screeching now.

"My shift is over."

"You don't have any loyalty or work ethic, Justin. You walk out that door and you're fired."

"No work ethic?" Justin growled, suddenly angry. "Look, you *fuck*, I trained for the motherfucking Olympics for years. Hours and hours every fucking day. I worked my ass off and I don't need a piece of shit asshat telling me about my work ethic!"

Rob looked like he was going to blow a vein, his face going beat red, his eyes bugging out. "You're fired!"

Jason flipped the bastard off. "Fuck off and die, asshole. I quit."

Rob stood there mouth opening and closing, face going even redder as clapping came from down the hall.

Coach stood there, smiling at him. "Well done, Justin. Come on. Let's go get some supper and celebrate your freedom."

He nodded, grabbed his favorite coffee cup, his briefcase, and left his key card on the desk.

Coach's hand slid against his lower back, leading him out to the street. "I'm so proud of you, Justin."

"I. I." He was going to lose it.

They went out to the car and Coach went on. "Seriously.

59

You stood up for yourself. That was fantastic."

Justin nodded. He'd quit his job. Oh, God.

Coach got them settled in the car and headed into traffic. "You going to freak out on me?"

"Nope." He was going to freak out totally inside his own head.

He was given a grin. "The restaurant isn't far. I think a celebration is in order."

"Okay." He'd quit his job. His job. He'd called his boss an asshat. While it was true, it wasn't something you said to the man's face.

"There's a Japanese place just around the corner."

"Cool." He was going to have to live in a shed somewhere.

Coach glanced at him, one eyebrow up. "You're way too calm."

"Told you I wasn't going to freak out on you." Nope. He was going to have a beer or six, get really, really drunk and possibly rant like a howler monkey, alone in his bedroom tonight.

"Well, now there's no reason for you not to take me up on that job offer."

"We'll see." He didn't know, still.

"What do you mean, we'll see? Why are you resisting this so hard?" Coach pulled into a parking garage, stopping to grab the ticket from the machine.

"I don't know if I can deal with the water and stuff."

"You mean being at the pool and not being the swimmer?"

"Yeah."

They parked and he slipped out of the car. He'd lost his job. He'd. Lost. His. Job.

Coach came around the car and put an arm around his shoulders. "Come with me on Saturday and we'll see how you do. The kids would be *thrilled* to have you there."

"Maybe. I don't have plans."

"I'm still trying to talk you into making plans to move into my place." They went into the restaurant, the air cool, Japanese music playing softly over the speakers.

"Oh, this is pretty." Calming. Probably what he needed right now as he'd just called his boss an asshat and quit!

"It is. I wanted someplace to woo you."

The hostess came over and welcomed them before showing them to a table in the window, affording them a view of the street.

He'd quit his job. "Woo me?"

"Talk you into moving in with me, into working with me, into being my boy."

"I...What did you do today?"

"Cleared out two drawers in my dresser and some room in my closet."

Oh. Oh, Chris did want him there. If only he knew for sure what to do.

"I found a couple of cooking courses running in the evenings, too. I thought we could do the first one together."

"A cooking class?" Him?

"Yeah. It's about time we knew how to make more than whatever we can dial up."

Justin didn't know about that. Still, it would be something to try.

Their waitress came and Coach ordered for both of them. "The sushi platter for two please, and a couple glasses of water."

He smiled at Chris. It was so nice, to be with someone who knew you. Coach didn't really look much older, in fact, now that Justin himself was older, Chris almost seemed younger. In his mid-thirties, Chris' eyes were as blue as ever, and still as sharp—Justin knew they somehow saw everything. Coach's hair was longer than he remembered it ever being, messy and in need of a cut.

The strong, swimmer's body was still toned, even though Justin knew that Chris hadn't swum competitively since high school. He knew what that body felt like against him now... He shook himself.

Chris looked at him, smiled like he knew.

"Stop it," Justin ordered.

"Stop what?" Coach did not do innocent very well.

"You know."

Coach raised his hands, palms out. "I'm just sitting here."

"Uh-huh." Justin pursed his lips. "I quit my job."

"You hated that job and your boss was a total asshole. Plus, you already have another job lined up. Looks like a sound decision to me."

"He *was* an asshole. I hate ties."

"You look much better in Speedos." Chris smiled as he said it, like he was imagining it.

"I don't own a pair anymore."

"What did you do with all the ones you had?"

"I sold them to collectors." It had been hard, at first.

Coach blinked at him. "All of them?"

"Yep. I needed tuition money."

"Tell me you didn't sell your medals."

He shook his head. "I put all of them except the Olympics golds in a museum."

Coach looked relieved. "I have a spot for them on my shelves at home. Waiting for you." The words were quiet, sincere.

"You can have them, you know." He'd offered them to Chris after he retired.

"They are yours and they'll go on the shelves when you move in."

"I earned them. I'm proud of them." He was. They were the best thing he'd ever done, probably that he'd ever do.

"You did earn them. Every single one. And I'm proud of you." Chris reached out and took his hand. "I love you."

"Don't say that. You don't know me anymore and I can't lose you again right now." He'd almost lost his mind before and now? He just couldn't.

"It's the truth and it means you aren't going to lose me again. Why would you think my loving you means you'll lose me?"

He shrugged, sighing when the water came. He'd hoped for sake or something; he just wanted to get drunk.

Chris' eyes were on him and as soon as their waitress left he leaned in. "You haven't answered me yet."

"I'm not going to."

Chris shook his head. "You'll eventually believe me, Just."

"Let's drink," he suggested. Coach could order the sake.

"To what?"

"To my unemployment."

"How about to new beginnings?" Coach picked up his water, not getting the clue about the sake.

He nodded. "That sounds much nicer, Coach."

Coach clinked their glasses together and took a sip of his.

Sake would have burned down his throat, tingled on his tongue. He thought about that and he tried not to think about what he'd done.

Their food arrived in short order, the plates of sushi so pretty. He finished his water, then started the complicated process of exactly the right ratio of wasabi to soy sauce. Coach watched him, not eating or drinking, just watching.

"What?"

"Love watching you eat." Coach kept saying that. "You've got a routine, you know?"

"Me?" Nonsense.

"Yes, you. Look at you with your condiments. It's always the same when you eat sushi." Coach's foot found his under the table, just resting them together.

"It has to taste good." Silly man.

"Most of us just do this." Coach grabbed a piece of salmon on rice and dipped it into the soy sauce before popping it into his mouth.

Justin shrugged. He liked what he liked.

"I'm not trying to change, just explaining why I enjoy watching you eat." Chris' foot rubbed his.

He thought about that for a second, then let himself relax. There wasn't any reason to get all caught up, not about this.

Chris grabbed a California roll and dipped it into his perfectly ratio of wasabi and soy sauce and then held it to his lips. "Open up."

He opened, the salt and burn perfect. Chris moaned softly, eyes on him.

"It's good." He licked his lips clean.

"Uh-huh." Chris sounded a little breathless.

"You should have one."

"I should." Chris leaned forward and opened his mouth.

He dipped a piece in Chris' soy sauce, fed his coach.

"Mmm." Chris pulled the sushi from his chopsticks and licked his lips. "It's good."

"It is." Justin relaxed back.

Chris snagged himself another piece. "I'm taking you home after we're finished dinner."

"Are you?" He loved how Chris was so sure of everything.

"I am. It'll be a better celebration with orgasms."

He looked at Coach, then chuckled.

"Trust me. I know about this." Coach grinned and

grabbed another piece of sushi.

"You think you know about everything." He chose a piece, too, nibbling.

"No, but I think I know about you, and about me."

Justin believed that. "No one ever knew as much about me."

"No one else ever will. I have a special interest."

He looked at Chris. "You make it sound so..." Special? Wonderful? Real? Something.

"It's the best thing in the world, Justin. And I'll telling you that until you believe it for yourself."

He didn't know what to say to that. Coach didn't push him to say anything, though, and they shared the rest of the sushi platter, their feet tangled together under the table. They finished their second glasses of water, and Justin was warm, buzzing just the barest bit from the food and attention.

"You want red bean ice cream for dessert, or are you ready to just go?"

"Let's go. I'm full and it's going to be an hour before we want anything else."

"Sounds good." Coach caught their waitress' attention and motioned for the check.

He pulled out some cash. "For my half."

"My treat, Just. It was my showing up that prompted your run-in with that dickwad boss of yours."

"It was long-time coming. It really was. I was getting irritated."

Coach nodded. "You didn't seem very happy there." That was an understatement.

The waitress brought their check and Coach handed over his credit card.

"I'm wasn't. I'm not a very happy go-lucky guy." He wasn't sure he'd ever been, but he thought he had. Once.

"You're happy when you have your routine." Coach's

smile was warm and directed right at him. "We'll get you there, Just."

"Do you really believe that?"

"That we'll get you there or that you're happy when you've got routine." Coach shook his head. "It doesn't matter, I *know* they're both true."

"I wish I could just believe that. Maybe I'll just believe in you. It used to work."

"That'll work as a start."

The waitress brought back Chris' credit card and slip, and Coach signed them, and pocketed his card. "Okay, Just. Let's go home."

"Can we go to your place?" He didn't want to face his roommate and his room.

"Our place. And sure. That is the plan, after all."

"Cool. Thank you." He just wanted something good for a few more minutes.

Coach grabbed his hand and led him out of the restaurant, all the way back to the car without letting go. He held on, humming under his breath. They got to the parking garage and up to the car, where Coach pulled him in close, took his mouth.

Oh. Oh! He jerked, surprised and turned on, all at once. The kiss was long and hard and they were both breathless when Chris' lips finally left his. Justin blinked, the whole world swaying. Wow.

Chris stroked his cheek, then opened the car door for him. "Let's take this home."

"Uh-huh." He sat, rubbed his cock, idly.

"Stop that. Number one rule. No touching yourself without my say-so." The words were casually spoken as Chris slid into the driver's seat.

"Wh...what?"

"You remember our conversation from the other night, don't you? Rule number one was no touching yourself.

Leave that cock alone."

"It's mine." He felt the words, in the pit of his belly.

Chris held his gaze now. "And you're mine, and it's a rule."

It was like electricity, a spark burning deep inside him. Chris had to have seen, because his nostrils flared and suddenly there was heat in his eyes.

"I don't follow rules anymore." He licked his lips, his muscles feeling like they were burning and jumping.

"And you're miserable. I know what makes you happy, J. Let me do it."

"You promise it'll work?"

"I promise." Coach still had his gaze, and he could see Chris was deadly serious.

He moved his hand away from his cock, fingers trembling.

"Good boy." The words were softly spoken almost gentle, but they echoed through the car.

He shivered, suddenly wanting to run or scream or burst into tears. Coach started up the car, heading toward Coach's house. Justin sat, trying his best to breathe. In. Out. In. What was he doing? Out. In.

"I want you to move in with me Just. I want you to work with me. I want us to make a life together."

"I can't take any more today, Chris." He went with as honest as he could be. "I can't change one more thing."

"Then simply come home with me and let me love on you."

"Yes, please."

"Excellent." Coach started the car and headed out toward his place.

The panic built slowly, like it used to before meets, a tickle at the base of his skull. Coach leaned over and turned on the radio hard driving metal pouring out of the speakers. His eyes closed and he nodded, that sound as familiar and comfortable as breathing. Coach's hand brushed his thigh, letting him know Coach was there with him. This was something he understood in a world that was confusing as hell.

They pulled up into the drive at Coach's house and the music fell silent as the engine was turned off. "Come on, Just. We're home."

"Okay." He felt a little like he'd blown a meet. "I'm sorry."

"For what?" Coach turned back and looked at him as they headed for the garage door.

"I don't know."

"Then you don't need to apologize." Coach opened the door but before they went in drew him close.

He stepped in, sucking up the comfort Coach offered him. Coach tilted his head up and took a kiss.

This had never been part of their thing, not before, but it felt so good, now. Chris' tongue slid into his mouth, touching his teeth, his gums, his own tongue.

His cock, which hadn't ever stopped paying attention, was heavy now, full, sliding on Chris' leg. Chris groaned, hands finding his ass and tugging him even closer, helping him rub. Oh. Oh, please. He pushed into the kiss, rocking a little harder.

Chris picked him right up, using the weight of his own body to add to the friction on his prick. It was all he could do, hips rolling as he cried out. Yes. Yes. Leaning back against the wall, Chris kept moving him, bringing him closer and closer.

Justin was gonna... right here in the garage. Chris wasn't slowing down any, the hand on his ass squeezing hard. His eyes closed and he let go, let his body move and rock and drive until he couldn't bear it another second.

Chris' mouth left his. "Come for me."

He shot, just like that, head back, throat working.

Chris latched onto his throat, pulling hard and making him shudder, stretching out his orgasm. He moaned, the pleasure going on and on, sweet as anything. Chris moved his mouth over, lips wrapping around a new spot.

"Coach. Fuck." That was hot.

Coach just hummed around his skin, making it vibrate. His knees were weak, his heart slamming in his chest, and he couldn't stop moaning. Coach started walking backward, in through the garage door. There he was pushed up against the wall, Coach pressing hard against him. He was swampy, his body trying to recover.

Coach's fingers wrapped around either side of his shirt and pulled it open. Buttons went flying and he would have complained, but it was too hot. Coach pushed the shirt over his shoulders and down his arms, trapping them against his sides, Coach's mouth never leaving his except to let them take short gasps of air.

He was on fire. On fire. Fuck.

Coach plucked at his right nipple, teasing it with alternating hard and soft touches. It was just starting to be normal, to not be swollen. Coach seemed intent on changing it back to swollen.

"Coach." He was going to bruise. Again.

"Huh?" Coach went down to bite at his nips.

"You'll leave marks." His toes curled. God. God, that throbbed.

"Yes."

"You can't. They'll ache." His cock was filling again.

"Yes," Coach said again, pinching his right nipple hard.

"Fuck!" He went up on tiptoe.

"Eventually." Coach gave him a grin, tugging on his other nip.

"You have to stop..." He groaned, then wrinkled his nose. "I need to clean up."

"We'll shower in a minute." Coach took his right nipple in and began sucking.

"I..." Fuck. Fuck, that was intense. He felt each and every pull, balls deep.

Coach wasn't stopping, either. No, if anything, the suction was getting stronger. These sounds started leaving him, tearing from him. He felt that everywhere. Then Coach's teeth closed over the very tip of his nipple, biting. He screamed, the sensation overwhelming, sharp. Perfect. Coach's smile pulled at the edges of his skin, and then the hurt was soothed by a hot tongue.

The room was spinning and he was shaking, cock hard again. Coach finally let go of his nipple, the air hitting it hard, surprisingly cold. Then Coach headed it right for his other nipple. He shifted away, shook his head, hand hiding his nipple. Coach growled—growled!—at him.

"Coach!"

"I'm going to make it a rule, Justin. You never, ever hide your nips from me."

He covered the other one, too. "A rule?"

Coach growled again, and took his hands, pulling them away. "No hiding your nips from me. Or you will be punished."

"You can't." He couldn't quite breathe.

"Is that a challenge?"

"I'm not going to let you." He was achingly hard.

"You aren't going to have a choice." Coach leaned in and bit his left nipple.

"H...hey!" Oh, God. He was burning up.

"Right here." Coach grinned and snapped his teeth in the air just over his other nipple. He pulled away, stepped away, heart racing. Coach grabbed his hand. "Okay. Shower, bed, and if you're very good, making love."

"I..." He shivered, nodded, so close to melt down it was crazy.

Coach wasn't waiting for him to say more, striding down the hall with him in tow. He stumbled along behind Chris, heart pounding. He dropped his shirt off his arms, the thing dangling from his wrist where Chris had his hand and refused to let go until they reached the bathroom. He toed off his shoes, hurrying to get his nasty pants and briefs off.

"I made you cream your jeans." Coach looked awfully proud of himself.

His cheeks burned and he ducked his head, embarrassed.

Coach cupped his cheek and tilted his head back up. "I made you come in your pants; that's not anything to be ashamed of. It's something to revel in."

He swallowed hard, then just pushed back into Chris' arms. He needed touch. Chris' mouth dropped down on his, the kiss hot and hard and whipping everything else away. He sobbed into the kiss, shattered, overwhelmed. He had trusted this man with everything, his whole life.

"I have you," whispered Chris.

He nodded. Good. Good. He needed that right now. More kisses followed, Chris making his head swim.

Somehow they were in the shower together, naked, hot water making things fuzzy. Chris' hands soothed and excited him, sliding on his body and touching him everywhere. His nerves and worries faded, and he could breathe, touch Chris back. Eventually, Chris leaned him up against the tile, taking kiss after kiss from him. Justin gave them, moaning and sighing happily with every kiss.

"Sensual. Sexy. Amazing boy."

"Coach. So good."

"That's what I want to hear." Coach took his mouth again.

Justin could happily drown in Coach's kisses. He stayed close, each kiss making him that much more solid.

Coach rubbed against him, cock hard on his belly. He reached down, stroking Chris, gently, slowly, just wanting to give the man pleasure.

"Mmm." Chris hummed into the kiss, hand coming up to curl around his hip. They rocked together, his hand continuing to pet, to stroke, to love on Chris.

Chris' other hand slid along his side, and then found his nipple, thumb rubbing across it. The ache was deep, down in his belly, but his relaxation was bigger. A little pinch tweaked his nipple and Chris sucked on his tongue. He gripped Chris' cock, fingers rubbing the tip. Chris jerked for him, fingers pinching his nipple again.

"Coach..." He shook his head, pulled back.

The hand around his hip slipped around to grab his ass and pull him back in. He was shaking, just the littlest bit, but everywhere.

"I have you," Chris told him, eyes meeting his.

"I'm just... You know."

"You just need to trust me and I know you know how to do that."

"I do. I do trust you."

"Then we're golden."

He chuckled. "I was, once upon a time. Do you remember?"

"You still are to me, Justin." Coach looked him right in the eye as he said it, not an ounce of guile there.

He reached up, cupped Chris' cheeks. Chris just kept looking right into him. He had no words. None.

"I love you, Justin. I want you here with me. I want you by my side."

He leaned in, brought their lips together. Chris opened up, sucking on his tongue as soon as he slipped it into Chris' mouth. That wasn't as lazy, easy. This time the kiss made his abs tight. Humming like he knew Chris made the kiss even deeper. Justin moaned, let himself slide on

Chris' body. God, he wanted.

One of Chris' hands slid around his body, sliding along his crack. He wasn't sure whether to push back or pull in. Chris took the choice from him, fingertip breaching him.

"Oh." He wasn't sore anymore, but the touch was still unfamiliar, surprising.

"So hot." Chris' voice was low, rough and needy.

"Uh-huh." He was. He felt like he was burning up.

Coach grabbed the body wash and poured it into his hand, then that finger was back, slippery and slick, pushing into him He rocked, the slippery, strange burn exciting as fuck. Chris' finger pushed deep inside him and he could feel it moving, pushing at his insides. His abs tightened and he stretched.

Another finger pushed into him, stretching him more as Chris insisted it could go in too. His nipples went hard, aching on his chest. Then a third finger pushed into him, stretching him wide. He gasped softly, warning Chris that he was full.

"You'll take my whole hand one day."

"No way." That was impossible.

"Yes. But not today. Today you'll take my cock." Chris' fingers hit his gland as he said it.

Justin jerked, bucked forward. Lightning. That was like lightning. Groaning, Chris latched onto his mouth and then did that thing with his fingers again. His eyes rolled and he shook. Oh, fuck. Again. Chris obliged his silent plea, fingers pushing into that spot again and again, tongue fucking his mouth with the same rhythm. His cock ached, his ballsac tight, and he was going to shoot. He had to.

The kisses ended and Chris leaned in to wrap hot lips around his neck. The pressure inside him grew and he whimpered, his cock leaking, dripping as Chris worked him.

"You've already come," murmured Chris. "You wait for me to be fucking you before you do it again."

"You..." Those fingers didn't stop moving, stroking him inside, over and over.

"There will be nipple clamps if you come before then."

"You have to stop touching!" His thighs spread, body lifting on tiptoe.

"I have to make sure you're stretched enough to take my cock." That touch didn't stop, the fluttering caress inside him making him sob.

Coach's fingers stretched and twisted together, but always pushed in against that spot. It didn't even feel like a real orgasm when he came, but spunk poured out of him, spilling on Chris' thigh.

"Damn, Just. Now I'm going to have to punish you." Coach really didn't have to sound quite so fucking pleased about it.

He shook his head. "You... you did that."

"Semantics. I'm still using the clamps on your nipples when we're done in here." Coach's fingers slid out of him.

His knees buckled a little, his body so empty, nerves firing. Coach moved him, turned him to face the wall, the big, solid body behind him, hard cock rubbing his ass. His entire body bucked, hips rocking instinctively.

"Needy boy. I'm coming." Coach reached for something just outside the shower.

"Coach." He shook his head, sucked in one breath after another.

"Just getting a condom, J."

He nodded, trying to put his thoughts together. Coach was up against his back again before he could take a few breaths.

"Can't wait to be inside you again."

"You liked it?"

Coach's hand slid along his back. "Fucking loved it."

He liked how that sounded. "Good."

"Yeah. Very." Coach shifted his legs, and the strong hands spread his ass.

He groaned, hands sliding on the tile.

"Gonna be inside you, Justin." Coach pushed, the thick cock pressing hard against his hole and then spreading him.

Justin moaned, that stretch sweet, almost comforting now.

"Oh, fuck. Justin. So fucking tight." Chris kept pushing in, taking him.

He reached up, hands going high over the tile. Pushing forward until he was pressed against the wall, Coach was good and solid behind him. That cock was so deep it seemed to fill him totally, spread him, pierce him. Then Coach wiggled a little and brushed his gland. He cried out, the sound shocked.

"There," growled Chris, pushing into him and hitting it again.

"Coach!" His cock tried to fill again, impossibly.

"That's right, babe." Coach nailed that spot again.

He was trapped between the wall and his lover, and there was nowhere to go. Coach set up a quick pace, pushing into him and lighting his body up every time. All he could do was ride it, go with it. When Coach's hand pushed between him and the wall , grabbing his prick, he was almost shocked to realize he was hard again.

"I can't. I can't again." His body went tight.

"You can. This time with permission. On my order."

He shook his head. No way.

"Oh, yes. You will, Justin. You always did follow my orders." Coach's thumb pressed against his slit. The little sting was sweet, sharp, and his eyes crossed. Coach groaned. "I felt that."

"Huh?"

Coach pressed his slit again, lighting up his whole body. "When I do that you ripple around my prick."

He made a low, hungry sound, shivered.

"Mmm. Felt that, too." Coach jerked into him a few more times, hitting his gland, the double assault of cock and fingers almost too much.

He started crying out, over and over, moaning and calling for Chris.

"Yes. Justin. My boy. Mine." Chris' hand tightened on his cock, working him faster, harder.

He shook, caught, crying out Chris' name, over and over.

"Okay, Justin. Fuck. Come on now. Come for me. Come. For. Me." Each word was accompanied by a thrust.

He screamed, hands slamming on the tile as his cock pulsed. Coach froze behind him, moaning loudly. Before he collapsed, Chris grabbed him, held him.

"That's it, babe. My beautiful boy." Soft kisses landed his shoulders.

"I'm so tired." He held on, breathing deep. "Please. Let me stay." He knew Coach had said so, but his brain was just overwhelmed.

"You're staying." Coach slipped out of him and turned off the water before half-carrying out of the shower and wrapping a towel around him.

Soon he was in Chris' bed, held close, his world soft, protected.

"Love you, Justin." The words followed him into his dreams.

Chapter Six

Chris woke with his arms full of Justin.

Man, he could get used to this—he was going to get used to this, because Justin was going to move in with him. It was where the man belonged, after all. Justin needed unlike anyone he'd ever seen, trusted him, loved him. It was sexy. It was hot. It was arousing. It made him feel like everything was as it should be.

Justin murmured softly, nuzzling him.

"Yeah, babe." He slid his hand along Justin's spine.

"Coach. Love." Justin kissed his jaw, then dozed back off.

He beamed, though. Justin had called him love. His boy knew, in his heart, what was what. Thank god for the strength that let Justin call him, let him in.

Chris began touching, his fingers already addicted to the feeling of Justin's skin. His boy moaned, rocking gently against him. Humming happily, he slid one hand around so he could play with Justin's sensitive little nipples. Justin rumbled, curled in to protect them. He insisted, though. Really, they should always be swollen, bruised. It needed to be a rule.

Justin was going to be topless a lot. If they were always swollen and dark, it wouldn't seem odd. He slid down Justin's body, dropping a kiss on one shoulder before zeroing in on those sweet little nubs. Justin's hands moved to hide them, his boy still asleep. He took Justin's wrists and pulled his hands up over his boy's head.

Those beautiful bright blue eyes popped open. "Coach?"

He smiled into Justin's eyes as he transferred both wrists to his left hand. "Morning."

"M...morning." Sweet, confused boy.

He ignored the sweet nipple in front of him in favor of taking Justin's mouth in a good morning kiss. Justin groaned, kissing him lazily, still mostly asleep. He kissed Justin until he was breathless, and then he moved down to take Justin's right nipple into his mouth, sucking hard and working the blood to the surface.

"I... Oh."

That was right. *Feel it.*

He scraped with his teeth and then flapped his tongue back and forth across the tip, never letting up the suction.

"Chris. Chris, you can't..." Justin was starting to rock now, hips rolling against him. Like his boy wouldn't be terribly disappointed if he stopped.

He sucked even harder.

"Aches..." Justin pulled at his hand, muscles rippling.

He didn't let go of Justin's hands, but he did switch nipples. He bit and sucked, then bit again, tugging hard. He got to clamp these today, maybe he'd spend a few sessions with them, make them so sensitive. Pulling a leg around Justin, he pulled his boy into him, giving that writhing body someone to rub against.

Justin made the sweetest noises, deep and raw, cock leaving wet trails on his belly. He hummed around Justin's nipple, vibrating the now super-sensitive skin.

"Stop. Chris. Coach. Oh, fuck." Justin pushed harder.

He bit the tip of Justin's nipple, fairly hard. Justin jerked, spunk covering his belly. He rubbed their bellies together, the slick making everything glide and slide.

Justin moaned, shivering against him, eyes stunned.

He let go of his boy's hands and grinned. "Good morning."

"I. Morning. You. Damn."

He grinned, utterly pleased to have made Justin entirely incoherent.

"How are you so awake?"

Chris made the only reply that made sense. "I have a beautiful man in my bed, why wouldn't I want to be awake for that?"

"It's early."

Chuckling, he rubbed his prick against Justin's body. He wasn't sleepy. He wanted to play. They had two days before they had to be at the pool with the kids, and he wanted Justin back in the water before that.

"You wanna help me out here?" He rubbed again, his prick leaking on Justin's skin. He knew his boy. There wasn't a selfish bone in Justin's body. Spoiled, sure. Temper, Christ on a crutch. But not selfish.

Justin reached down, cupped his cock.

"Mmm." He pushed into Justin's touch as he pressed their mouths together.

Justin worked him, fingers sure, confident, touch enough to cross his eyes. He slid his own hand up, eager to feel the lovely heat of Justin's abused nipples.

"Don't. Don't touch."

He met Justin's gaze and grabbed one of the little tits.

"They ache."

"Good." He tugged on Justin's nipple. "I want them to."

Justin grabbed his hand. "Stop it."

"No, I don't think so." He grabbed Justin's nipple with the fingers of his other hand.

"Stop! No touching! I'll be thinking about them all the time!"

He nodded. Yeah, that worked for him. He tugged on Justin's nipple again, hard.

Justin pulled away, hands over his nipples. "I said stop. Fuck, man. You're making me crazy."

Chris grabbed Justin's hands and pulled them away from those lovely nipples. "That's the idea. But we can just start with the clamps instead."

"No way."

Oh, yes. No denying him access to those nipples. It was a rule. "I promised you this punishment for coming without permission last night."

"You made me."

"I encouraged you. Didn't make you." He moved over Justin, searching through the little drawer in the bedside table.

Justin moved away from him. "You did too."

"It's semantics, anyway." He found a pair of clamps and moved back to straddle Justin.

Justin twisted, giving him his back. "No."

He leaned down and spoke against Justin's spine. "You know you want it, Just. You want to know I see you, that I love you and will give you what you need."

Justin stilled, shivered, hearing him.

"Let me do this for you. For us."

"Coach."

He waited, petting, gentling, waiting Justin out until his boy turned. He rewarded Justin with a long, deep kiss. Justin was trembling like a leaf in the wind.

"I have you," he told Justin, his fingers finding Justin's right nipple, making sure it was good and hard, reaching for his touch, for the clamp about to come.

"I don't want to do this." Justin's nipple was rock hard.

"You do. You want me to tell you I love you. And I do. And you want me to do this." He put the first clamp on Justin's right nipple.

The clamp wasn't vicious, wasn't sharp at all, but still Justin arched up, then reached for it.

"No touching." He growled the words out, but didn't stop Justin's movements—his boy needed to obey on his own.

"It hurts."

He bent and blew on the clamped nipple. "It's a good ache, though." He didn't phrase the words as a question.

"I..." Justin shook his head, abs rolling.

"The other one now." He flicked the free nipple a few times, but it was already hard and reaching for the clamp, so he slid it right on.

"Take them off!"

"In fifteen minutes." He circled Justin's clamped nipples with his fingertips.

"I'm going home. Right now."

"You're staying right here. We'll go back to your place to get your stuff later." He wanted Justin home—home here. Now.

"I'm not!" That temper flared. "Fuck! I want them off!"

He leaned in and took Justin's mouth, pulling the words right into himself. He held Justin's hands, keeping his boy stretched, long. Running his free hand along Justin's side, he teased around the sweet nipples again. Justin screamed into his lips, legs kicking. That was it. Justin needed to let it all out. All of it.

He held on. He helped build the muscles in this body, studied it religiously for years. He knew it. He circled the other nipple, his legs holding Justin down.

"Leave me alone!" Justin was hard as nails, rubbing against him.

"Never again."

"Liar." Justin looked at him, though, so hopeful.

He just held Justin's gaze and shook his head. "I don't

lie to you, Justin."

"I hated you."

He knew. "I know." He didn't look away.

"I don't know what to do, Coach."

"You come home, Justin. Where you belong."

Justin looked so young, so vulnerable. "I want to."

"We can go pick up your stuff later today. I'll show you the pool I'm working at later, too." Get his boy in the pool; that would remind Justin of where he belonged.

"Okay." The word was just a whisper, so tired.

Together they were going to find Justin's joy again. Swimming. Routine. As much love as Justin could stand.

Bending, he kissed Justin softly, careful not to touch the clamped nipples. Justin cried for him, tears slipping from the pretty eyes.

He broke their kiss to lick the tears away. "Love you, Justin. My boy."

Justin took a long, shuddering breath. He kept licking, tongue tracing Justin's lips now. He kept murmuring, telling Justin how long he'd waited, wanted, whispering little praises. He glanced at the clock. Only a few minutes left until he took the clamps off. He'd be surprised if doing that alone didn't make Justin come.

He upped the ante, though, wanting this to be good, wanting to overwhelm the upset with need, so he reached down, fingers stroking Justin to full aching hardness.

"You're allowed to come," he told Justin. His boy would learn to wait for the permission, would crave being made to wait and prove himself.

"I already did once."

"You will again." He was sure of it: Justin had never felt anything like the clamps coming off his tits.

Chris kept stroking, kept kissing, keeping Justin off balance. When the fifteen minutes were up, he let Justin know. "The clamps are coming off now—you did great."

"Take them off." Justin looked a little desperate.

"I said just I would."

He watched Justin's face as he reached for the first clamp and removed it. The shock was delicious, those blue eyes wide, lips parted, not even a gasp leaving Justin. Bending, Chris wrapped his lips around the abused flesh, sucking, encouraging the blood to come back into Justin's nipple. Soft, near hysterical cries filled the air.

He rubbed the tip of Justin's prick and then murmured. "The other one now." He took the second clamp off with his teeth.

"*No!*" Justin pulled away, hands covering those poor nipples.

He jacked Justin hard. "Yes. Come on now, feel it all and come." He leaned in, bit Justin's earlobe. "Gonna punish you, boy. No hiding those nips from me. Ever."

Heat poured over his fingers. He groaned, the scent of Justin's need fucking arousing. He pushed against Justin, humping one of those strong thighs.

"Fuck. Fuck!" With that cry, he came, spunk pouring out over Justin's skin.

His boy was sobbing, holding onto him, trembling hard. He collapsed next to Justin and pulled his boy into his arms, supporting and loving Justin. The storm was fast, and soon he had an exhausted boy again. He shook his head. Justin had always needed structure. Now his boy was going to get it again, was going to thrive.

He pressed a kiss to the corner of Justin's right eye. "Nap, boy."

"Uh-huh. My head hurts, Coach." He got a sigh, then his boy just melted. "Love you."

Then the snores started.

Chris kissed Justin's forehead and held onto his boy as he slept, so in love it hurt.

Thank god, Justin had come back to him.

Chapter Seven

Justin woke up to the smell of eggs and grapefruit juice and toast, and for a second he was confused. That was the smell of every training morning.

"Hey, Justin. You coming back to the land of the living?" Coach stood at the doorway, tray in his hand, two plates on it. "Don't get used to the breakfast in bed service, though."

"I... what time is it?" It had to be late afternoon, from the look of the sun outside the window.

"About two. I figured you needed the sleep." Coach put the tray on the bed, two plates full of eggs and toast there, along with thin slices of ham and two glasses of juice.

"Are we going to the pool?" He sat up, hissing as the sheet slid down his nipples.

Coach's eyes went to his chest, a soft moan sounding. "Yeah. After 'breakfast'."

"It looks good." He looked at his chest, his nipples dark, swollen, sensitive. God.

"They're stunning." Coach's fingers slid around but didn't touch his nipples. "We'll always keep them like this."

"What?" His cock went hard and he wriggled, groaned.

"I think you heard me: these are going to be kept just

like this: pretty and red and swollen."

He shook his head. "I can't. I... The eggs look good."

Coach chuckled and handed him a fork. "Eat, lover."

"Thanks." He was ravenous and he had missed Chris' eggs, so he ate heartily, feeling more able to cope when his plate was cleaned than he had in months.

Coach ate more slowly, and he could feel the man watching him, smiling.

"You make the best eggs."

Coach grinned at him. "You've always been the only one who thinks I can cook anything."

He shrugged. "I like your eggs."

Coach leaned in and took a kiss. He kissed his lover, his coach, his oldest friend, right back. Moaning, Coach cupped his jaw and the kiss went long before Chris slowly backed off. He blinked, watched, hands itching to slide over the broad shoulders, the strong pecs. He simply licked his lips, though, not sure what the plan was.

"Okay. If you're done eating, we'll go hit the pool. I want you to have a chance to get a feel for the water before you start helping me out with the kids."

"I don't really swim anymore." He nodded, though, got their plates.

"That's just crazy." Coach went through his drawers and pulled out a couple pair of swimming trunks. One was offered over. "I'll trade you for the dishes."

"I just felt bad about it." He took the suit. "Do you want to wear them or just bring them?"

"We can change at the pool."

"'kay." He got his slacks on. "Do you have a t-shirt I can borrow?"

"Yep. First drawer, take whichever one you like. I'll be right back." Coach slipped out with their dishes.

"Thanks." He grabbed a t-shirt, hissing as he pulled it over his sensitive nipples.

The shirt smelled like Coach, though. He held the bottom to his face, just breathing Coach in.

"You find a t-shirt okay?" Coach's voice faded away.

He looked up, cheeks burning. "Uh-huh."

Coach smiled at him and came over, kissed him softly. He let himself lean and soak up the sure, strong presence.

"Fuck, I've missed you." Coach leaned their foreheads together.

"Yeah. Yeah, Coach. So much." He met those warm, brown eyes. "So much."

Coach looked into him for a long moment, holding him in that gaze as surely as in those arms. "Come on, Just. The water is calling for you."

"Is it? Are you sure?" He had to grin, though. He did love the water.

"Absolutely sure. You think it doesn't miss you as much as you miss it?" Coach led them down the hall and into the garage, stopping for them to slip on sandals.

"You have my old shoes?" God, they felt so normal.

Coach shrugged. "They were in my bag when we got home from the Olympics."

"I love these." He wiggled his toes. "Man, I am throwing these slacks away." Stupid work pants.

"Smart move. We can go pick up your clothes after the pool." Coach clicked his key fob, the car doors unlocking.

"My roommate's going to be so pissed."

"Tell him you'll pay him a month's rent in lieu of notice. I'm sure it'll soothe the sting."

"I hope so." He wasn't one hundred percent sure he cared.

It didn't take long to get to the pool and as soon as he stepped out of the car, the smell hit him. He stopped, just a little wigged out, a little freaked. Then Coach's hand slid along his spine and settled in the small of his back. "You belong here, Justin. Never forget that."

"I used to. Is it so weird for everyone?"

"I don't know, Justin. You're my only Olympian." That hand put some pressure, right there above his ass. "Come on. Once you're in the water it'll feel like coming home."

"Promise?"

"I do." God, that confidence was sexy. *That* brought him right home all on its own, too.

The pool was private, beautiful, and they were on their own. Justin was stripping down, moving into his suit without even thinking, his brain on autopilot. When he was done, he looked up to find Coach watching him, then Chris smiled, nodded and pointed at the water.

His body knew this—like he knew how to breathe, how to sleep. He stood at the edge and dove in.

Watching Justin swim was still one of the most beautiful things Chris had ever seen. He didn't even bother changing into his own suit to join Justin, preferring instead to sit on the bleachers and just watch. Every now and then he'd yell at Justin to stop favoring his left arm or to kick straighter, but on the whole, muscle memory did its thing and Justin flew through the water like he was born for it.

Which, of course, Justin was. The man needed to swim. Needed this. Maybe even more than the rules and the discipline and the order. Of course, put them all together and Justin would be a happy camper.

Chris glanced at the clock at the end of the pool. An hour had passed and Justin hadn't been working out. His swimmer would be sore tomorrow, if he wasn't careful. He whistled five times, counting on that to be ingrained as well.

Sure as life, Justin's head popped up at the edge of the pool. "Coach?"

It gave him a hard-on.

"That's it for today. You don't want to be too sore to swim tomorrow."

"Tomorrow?" His boy nodded, hauled himself up, breathing hard. "Okay, Coach."

Look at that. Just the promise of more swimming had Justin looking forward to tomorrow. His lover was made for this.

He tossed Justin a towel. "You can get a shower when we get home." They could take one together.

"Okay." Justin's hands were shaking a little. "Are we going to get my clothes?"

"Yes, we are. You have anything else you need?" If they could get everything in one trip...

"I don't have a lot of shit. My medals, my TV, X-Box. Laptop."

"We should be able to fit that in the car. Come on." He put an arm around his boy once Justin had pulled on his t-shirt and changed out his trunks for his slack, then led Justin back out to the car.

He could feel Justin's muscles, jerking and rolling, twitching.

"I'll give you a rub down when we get home, too. Buy you an orange juice on the way out, too." He lead the way, stopping in the lobby for the juice out of the vending machine.

"You don't have to. I mean, I'm not your swimmer anymore."

"You're my assistant coach now." He handed over the juice. "And my lover. It's my job to take care of you."

"I don't know if I'd be a good coach."

"Assistant coach." Chris winked at him. "And you'll be great. The kids'll just be happy having you in the pool with them."

Justin shrugged, smiled. "We'll see."

"Yeah, we will."

They got back into the car and he headed for Justin's old apartment. "How'd the water feel?"

"Good. Real good." Justin leaned back, eyes closed. "Familiar. I don't know."

"You looked good." For someone who hadn't been swimming in four years, Justin looked amazing.

"Thanks. It was a little weird, maybe."

"Weird? How so?" He would keep Justin talking about swimming. About the water.

"I just haven't, you know? I haven't been in the water much. Not the pool at all."

"You belong there. Even if it's just to do laps to work out. I have never seen anyone move in the water like you do." He wasn't blowing sunshine up his boy's ass, either. It was totally true.

He hated that snort, that unhappy sound Justin answered him with. "I'm just me."

The words made him growl. "We should all be as 'just; you as you are."

Justin's hand snuck over, touched his thigh, the tiniest, most gentle little caress. He shot Justin a glance and hummed softly. They were almost at Justin's old place.

"Are you sure you want to do this?" Justin asked, voice quiet.

"One hundred percent, Justin. I've never been more sure of anything." He pulled up into a visitor's spot at the apartment complex and turned to his boy. "Never."

"Never." Justin nodded. "Okay. I trust you."

"This is our lives—it's too important to bullshit you about."

"Okay. Let's go. I guess we need to do this."

"It's a good thing, Justin." He got out and followed Justin up the stairs. He wasn't letting his boy change his mind.

The apartment was a fucking nightmare. Filthy and stinky, cheap furniture and debris was everywhere. Christ, is this how Justin had been living? It made him growl again, though he kept this one under his breath. "Your room?"

"I'm at the end of the hall." Justin picked through the mess, led him to a sight that was weirdly familiar. Justin's bedroom was neat, simple, almost sterile.

The gold medals were on the dresser, along with a TV, an X-box, and a computer. Better. This was what his boy needed; the other rooms had to drive Justin crazy.

"Okay. Backpacks? Suitcases? Boxes? Bags?"

"I have a suitcase and my two big duffels." Justin's dresser was organized, one drawer filled with movies and magazines.

Chris took another look around and nodded. "That just might do it."

"I don't have a lot of stuff. I spend my cash on other stuff."

His eyebrows drew together. "What other stuff?"

"Booze, mostly. Online video games."

"Well, you're done with the booze." He went to Justin's closet and found the bags and the suitcase. Pulling them out, he tossed them onto the bed.

"I'm legal." Justin packed quickly, socks and jeans and t-shirts.

He chuckled. "That's not the point."

"It's not?" His boy looked so confused.

"No. It's not. You don't need the booze."

"I just take the edge off."

"I have plenty of ways for you to take the edge off." He went over to Justin and took his boy's shoulders. "It's a rule. No booze."

"A rule?"

He'd already talked to Justin about rules, but he had

a hunch they'd have to go over it again. And probably again and again. "Yes. A rule. You had them when you were my swimmer and you'll have them now. Now get back to packing." He started throwing stuff into one of the duffel bags.

"I. Okay." Justin unhooked X-box, TV, DVD player. Justin was going to thrive with him, with order and rules and lots of love.

Chris heard the door open, heard girls giggling, laughing. "Sounds like your roommate's home."

"Yeah." Justin sighed. "I guess I should tell him."

"Let's get the last of your stuff and then we can tell him together. Sounds like he has some company to help soften the blow of losing a roommate."

"I guess so, yeah." Justin sighed again, rubbed the back of his neck.

"Hey." He went over to Justin and took a hard kiss. "You're doing the right thing for you." He drew Justin in close, pressed their bodies together. "And for me. I am overjoyed that you're coming home."

He loved that grin, the one that said he'd touched Justin's soul.

"Come on. We're almost done." He gave Justin another quick, hard kiss.

"Uh-huh. I won't miss this place."

"No I imagine not." He hated it and he'd only been here five minutes, he could only guess how it had been just one more thing Justin didn't like about his life.

They gathered the last of Justin's things into the bags. It wouldn't take more than two trips to get everything, including the TV, into the car. His boy hadn't been living. He'd been... sticking around.

Chris grabbed Justin's TV and one of the duffel bags and headed out, following his boy.

There was a tall blond kissing a lovely girl—her bikini

clad body barely hidden. "Justin? Where you going, man?"

Justin shrugged. "I'm moving out."

"Making a change for the better," Chris put in.

"Cool." The guy didn't seem that put out. "No offense, man, but you've stopped hanging out."

Chris let his eyebrows go up. "Was that a part of the lease agreement?"

"Well, kinda. I mean, beer's expensive." God, this kid was a real treat.

Justin rolled his eyes. "What do I owe you?"

"So, what? You're just going?"

"That's right, he's just going." Chris was not going to let this kid make Justin feel bad over leaving. There were a million kids this guy could find to share partying expenses with.

"Dude, I need next month's rent. That's not cool."

"I'll give it to you, when I get my last pay check."

The kid's eyes went wide. "You got fired? Shit."

"Tell you what." Chris reached into his pocket and pulled out his wallet, found one of the loose checks that he kept for just this kind of occasion. "Let me just pay you what Justin owes now."

Justin protested. "You can't, Coach."

"Coach? You're going back to swimming? Are you smoking dope?" This asshole was cruising for Chris to smash his face in.

Justin stared. "No!"

"Jesus Christ, just tell me how much Justin owes you and we'll get out of your hair." He shot Justin a look. "You and I can talk about how you'll pay me back later."

The kid crossed his arms. "Six hundred will cover everything."

Justin groaned.

"His half of the rent is six hundred a month? For this place? Really?"

"Yep. Rent and utilities." That was a hell of a belligerent look. Frankly, it would be worth it just to get his boy away from here.

"I'll pay you, man, okay? I have the money." Justin rolled his eyes.

"You can pay me back, Justin." He was insisting on this. He wrote out the check, passing it over to Justin's roommate to fill in the 'to' line. "This way you're done here."

"We're having a big party next Friday, man, if you want to come."

Chris didn't say anything, waiting to see how his boy would respond.

Justin shook his head. "I... I don't... I think I got plans."

"I think you do, too." He smiled at Justin and nodded at the bags and stuff. "Let's get the car loaded."

"Okay. Okay, yeah. See you, man."

"I'll call. I think Marc's looking for a bigger room." Clearly Justin's former roommate had already moved on. It really was all about the shared expenses and partying with this kid.

They got the car loaded up and Chris waited while Justin returned the keys.

Starting the car, he headed for home. "You good?"

"I guess." Justin was looking at his hands.

He knew that look. "Talk to me, Just."

"There's nothing to talk about."

Right. Bondage. Need. A new love. Swimming. Losing his job. Moving. Nothing to talk about. Chris snorted. "There's plenty to talk about."

Justin shook his head. "I'm cool."

He'd always hated that. Always. He growled a little bit. "Don't lie to me."

"I'm not lying."

"You can't honestly tell me you're cool."

"Sure I can. Like a cucumber. Icy, even."

He snorted again.

"Stop snorting at me." Was that a growl?

"Then stop telling me how cool you are about every damn thing in your life right now, how you don't need to talk about anything."

"What the fuck do you want?"

He pulled into the drive and hit the button for the garage door opener. Once he'd stopped the car, he turned to Justin to answer his boy. "Everything."

Justin rolled his eyes. "That doesn't mean anything."

"Yes, it does. I'm absolutely serious about it, too."

Justin just stared at him, those eyes almost wild. He could see the stress, the panic, the worry—all of them right there.

He pulled Justin to him, bringing their lips together. "I love you, J. Not just when you tell me things are cool—always."

"Everything's changing."

Yes, and he had Justin's back. "I know. It's a lot to take in and change is hard. But things weren't great before and I am right here. I'm going to make sure you not only survive the changes, but thrive on them."

"Why? Why not just find another swimmer and be like a hero again."

"Because I love you and that's got nothing to do with having a swimmer."

"What if I won't let you love me?"

He chuckled softly. "Babe, you don't have a choice on that. I *do*." He reached out, cupped Justin's jaw, thumb sliding on the stubbled skin as Justin leaned into him. "You don't have to fight this so hard, Justin. You deserve happiness as much as the next guy."

"I just feel lost."

That didn't surprise him. Chris had been lost without this man for a long time. "We'll find each other, okay?"

Justin looked at him, so serious, so quiet. "You've never been lost a second of your whole life."

"That's not true. You just never saw it."

"Where am I going to put my stuff?" The question was a not-so-terribly subtle change of subject.

"I told you I made room in my drawers and closet for your clothes. We can put your TV and gaming console in the den." He let the change of subject go and climbed out of the car, moving to start officially moving Justin in.

They got everything in, the unpacking painfully, almost embarrassingly simple. The X-box was hooked up, the duffels unpacked, and the movies added to his media shelf.

He showed Justin the place on his shelves that he'd cleared for the medals. "I'd be honored if you displayed them here."

"I was so proud of them. I slept with them, that first few months."

"Yeah?" He grinned. "That's cool. I'm still proud of you."

"I know." Justin put the medals up, the four of them shining, lovely.

He slid his arms around Justin, put his chin on Justin's shoulder. Justin took a deep, slow breath, and just relaxed back against him. That was it. His boy needed to trust him. He let the moment linger, let them both enjoy Justin being home. This is what he'd needed, ever since he'd watched Justin walk out of his life. He finally felt whole again.

"I love you." he spoke the words against Justin's skin.

Justin took a shuddering breath. "I want you to."

"Good. Because I do." He wrapped his lips around Justin's throat, began to suck up a mark.

He didn't bite, didn't pull hard. He wanted Justin to stay easy, stay melted back against him. His tongue worked Justin's skin, pulling the salt and sweat and chlorine taste. Justin hummed for him, rocking so slowly, like they were dancing. His hands slid down to cup Justin's hips, feeling the sharp bone beneath Justin's shorts. There were dark bruises there, ones shaped like his fingers. He scraped his teeth gently down along Justin's neck.

Justin moaned low, went up on tiptoe. "Fuck."

"That comes later. We need to shower first."

"I didn't mean... I wasn't asking."

He chuckled. "I was teasing, J."

"Oh. Duh."

He patted Justin's ass. "Come on, babe. Let's go shower."

"I'd love that." Justin turned, kissed him almost chastely. "Thank you for this afternoon. It felt so good."

He beamed at his boy. "I'm glad. I hope you have a lot more days where you say that."

"Me too."

Yes. That's what he wanted from Justin—for Justin to want more from his life.

He took Justin's hand and led him down the hall.

Chapter Eight

Justin woke up Friday morning before dawn, blinking, trying to figure out where he was, what he was doing. Chris grunted, rolled over, and everything came back to him in a rush. Christ. He'd moved in. With Chris. Chris who he was in bed with, Coach pushing closer, prick hard and hot against Justin's thigh. He couldn't help but smile, snuggle in and let their skin touch. Coach had had them in bed early, had loved him into oblivion and let him rest.

He couldn't remember the last time he'd woken up feeling this good, honestly.

Coach's arm slid across him.

"Mmm." His lips found Chris' throat, his hips pushing closer to that smooth, heated skin.

Chris' fingers slid over his hip and found his ass, curling into it, the touch hard enough to make him ache. He wasn't sure if Chris was awake or anything, but he kept touching, kissing and licking. Chris moaned for him, hips beginning a slow push against him. His body answered the motion, the blankets pulled around them, hiding the slowly lightening sky.

"Justin..." His name sounded like a prayer.

"Mmmhmm. So warm, Coach."

"For you babe."

He nodded, moaned, nibbled on Chris' collarbones.

"Love your mouth." Chris' fingers slid into his hair, cupping his scalp.

Golden

The little words made him ache, made him hard as hell. Chris' hands slid over him as the man arched up against him, wordlessly demanding more. Justin gave it, biting and licking, kissing and sucking. Each touch had Chris moaning, jerking, pushing into his hand or his lips. It was the easiest thing ever, to head south, to wrap his mouth around that fat, swollen cock.

"Oh, fuck! Babe..."

He hummed his pleasure, then relaxed, drawing Chris in, tongue sliding. Chris bucked, prick pushing deep before his hips settled back down on the bed. How hot, that he could make Chris need so much.

Chris' legs spread, hands sliding over his head and small, needy sounds came out of Chris. Justin just sucked, focusing on nothing but loving on his man.

"Yeah. Babe. Good. So good."

Every little bit of praise warmed him, made him try harder.

"Fuck. Gonna make me..."

He gently rolled Chris' balls. *Come on.*

"Justin!" Calling out his name, Chris came, spunk filling his mouth.

He sucked and groaned and swallowed, humming around Chris' prick. Chris jerked and shivered, the thick cock spurting a few more times before Coach went totally limp on the mattress.

Justin rested his cheek on Chris' thigh, reached down to jack himself off. He didn't need much, just a touch or two.

"Don't you dare touch that."

"Shh." He just needed a touch.

"Rule number one, babe. No touching. You get what you need from me."

"You're going to have to start writing them down."

Coach laughed. "I would think rule number one—no

touching your prick would be easy to remember."

"You're supposed to be sleeping."

"Not even a dead man could have slept through that blow job. Now come up here."

He crawled up Chris' body, rubbing the entire way.

"Cheeky," murmured Chris, bringing their lips together.

Now, he hadn't said anything. Nothing at all. Chris grabbed his ass and deepened the kiss. Justin pushed right into the kiss, lips opening to let Chris in. Chris' fingers slid over his belly, but instead of moving downward to his prick, Chris moved upward, toward his nips. He groaned, shook his head. They ached. That didn't stop Chris, though, the man's fingers sliding up to pick at his flesh.

"Coach." He moaned against Chris' lips, arching away.

"Right here and you're not going anywhere, either." Chris pinched his left nipple first, then the right.

He grabbed Chris' wrists.

Chris' eyebrows went up. "They need to be good and swollen, babe. All the time."

"Why?"

"Because I like them like that."

"But..." That didn't work. They'd drive him crazy.

"And if they're always dark, no one will know that's not how they come naturally. See? It's all good."

Justin shook his head, lips opening and closing. It was too early for logic. Chris half dragged him higher, half slid lower, and suddenly the man's lips were on his right nip, working it.

"Chris. Chris, stop." His hips were rocking, driving his cock against Chris' chest.

Chris didn't stop. If anything, Coach's suction got harder.

"You have to stop. I'll make you." His head fell back, his balls tight.

Chris finally did stop.

And then he moved to the other one, sucking on it.

He pushed Chris away, hands wrapping around his cock. "Fuck!"

"Justin!" Chris grabbed at his hand and tugged it up over his head. "No touching!"

"I need." He ached.

"Trust me to take care of you."

Oh. Oh, that was no fair. That made it his fault.

Still holding his wrist, Chris went back to sucking on his left tit.

"Let me go." He pulled, body sliding on the sheets.

"No." It was all Chris said before sucking harder, teeth teasing his skin.

The ache was maddening and he sobbed, twisting and fighting, caught. Free hand dropping to his prick, Chris wrapped around it as he kept sucking at Justin's nipple.

"Oh, fuck. I can't think. Shit." He humped, fucking Chris' hand.

"Told you I'd take care of you." Chris bit at his nipple, finger pushing into his slit.

Justin came so hard the room greyed out, his cries ringing out.

"Mmm. There you are." Chris' hand kept moving, slowly now, though.

All he could do was whimper. Chris swallowed the sound, mouth covering his. He shuddered, the pleasure still sparking along his spine. Tongue fucking his mouth, Chris kept moving against him. This was crazy. He couldn't think.

Chris rolled him, put him on his back. "Morning, babe."

"M...morning."

Chris grinned at him. "You ready to go do a few laps to start the day?"

"You're very awake."

"You very awoke me."

Justin cracked up. Chris' sense of humor had always been one of his favorite things on earth. The man could always make him laugh. Chris' smile made him happy, deep inside.

"I'd love to do some laps. Then, maybe we could have breakfast at Rosie's? It's Friday." They loved their lazy breakfasts.

"That sounds like the best idea." Chris kissed him, rubbed their noses together.

"It does." God, it so did.

Chris sat back with his beer, waiting for Justin to make his move on the checkerboard.

It had been a great day. They'd made love, fooled around together in the pool, had long, easy breakfast and watched a couple movies. He was feeling lazy and happy and just plain good.

Justin took another piece, then ate a grape, licking the juice off his finger. Chris' prick jerked. Damn, Justin was fucking sexy. Justin had looked good today in the water. Not world-class, but good. Good enough to wonder if maybe... He took his move, shaking his head at himself. Justin was retired, right? It had been his decision and it had been a good one. Right?

"Everything okay, Coach?"

"Yeah, I was just woolgathering." He gave Justin a smile. "You hungry? There's a new Chinese place I've been wanting to try."

"Sure. Sure. I love the sweet and sour stuff."

"I know." He remembered; he remembered everything about Justin.

Justin grinned. "And you like the beef and broccoli."

"I do. And those damn egg rolls." He could eat those until he exploded.

"With the sauce..." Justin groaned.

He chuckled. "Yeah. Let's see if this place lives up to our past favorites."

"Sounds good to me, Coach." Justin ate another grape, then one more.

He jumped three of Justin's checkers. "King me."

"Nope. Sorry. You're screwed."

He shot a look at Justin. "What?"

Justin chuckled. "I'm changing the rules. I get to keep your checker."

"You don't get to change the rules, babe."

"Sure I do." The tension, the arousal between them flared.

He met Justin's eyes. "Not how it works. I'm the coach."

"I'm just playing."

He held Justin's gaze. "I'm not."

"I..." Justin looked away, stood up. "I'll go get my phone so we can order supper."

He reached out and grabbed Justin's hand, tugged him into his lap. "This between us is real, it's good."

Justin stared at him. "I was just playing with you. I don't..."

"You don't what, babe?" Justin had to finish one of those sentences.

"I'm wigged."

Yes, he imagined so. He rubbed Justin's back. "It's been good, though, hasn't it?"

Justin nodded. "It has."

"Well, then." He kissed Justin softly. "How about we

go over the rules as they stand, see if we're going to add any others."

"We?"

"You're allowed to make suggestions, requests." This had to belong to both of them, not just him.

"I'm uncomfortable."

Chris thought that was part of the excitement, the rush. He stood, still holding Justin and moved them to the couch. "Now you're comfortable physically, even if you aren't mentally."

"Don't you want me to call for food?"

"Go ahead and call. That'll give us a timeframe for our discussion."

"Okay. Okay." Justin disappeared, and he heard the order being made. He'd been with other subs, leaning the ropes, trying things out, but they'd been practiced, almost blasé.

He preferred the honest responses he got from Justin. Hell, if he was honest—which he tried his damnedest to be—he loved the awkwardness, the nerves. He found a pad of paper and a pen by the time Justin had ordered their food and come back to him. He patted his lap. Justin stopped, looked at him, then came closer.

"How long is it going to be?" He wrapped a hand around Justin's wrist and tugged him down.

"Forty-five minutes."

"Excellent." He handed over the pen and paper. "You can write each rule down."

"I'm not sure about this whole rule thing."

"I am. Besides, there were plenty of rules when you were my swimmer."

"Yeah, but I was a swimmer, then."

"Well now you're my boy. And there will be plenty of rules." Because his boy thrived under rules. Because they would give Justin the structure he so desperately needed.

Because it would mean he saw Justin.

"I get to say yes or no, though."

"You can say anything you want. I won't necessarily take the rule back, though."

"God. Let's do this. Hurry up." That was his babe, rip the bandage off.

"Don't be pushy," he teased. At Justin's look, he chuckled. "Okay, okay. Rule number one is the same as it's always been. No touching your prick without my permission."

"I don't like that one." Justin wrote it down, though.

"It was the first one, though, and it'll always be the first one."

Justin shivered, and those muscled thighs shifted.

"Do you remember any of the others we've talked about?"

Justin blushed. "Not to hide my nipples, but I'm going to."

"Write it down. It's rule number two. We'll decide on punishments when we've gone through rules."

Justin's lips opened and closed, the look of shock delicious.

"Write it down, babe."

Justin's hand was shaking, but the words went down.

"Good boy." He stroked Justin's back, rewarding and soothing.

"This is crazy."

"No it isn't." And his boy was going to thrive because of it.

"Are we done?"

Oh, no. Not even close. "Nope. We've mentioned at least one more, haven't we?"

"What?"

"You are not allowed to run yourself down, Justin. Never. In fact, make that rule number one and move the rest down one, because this is the most important rule of all." He noticed that Justin didn't argue about that one. At all. "And in number two put respect the Dom. That's me and you can put Coach instead of Dom if you prefer."

"I respect you!"

"Yes, but if it's a rule and you're bucking for a punishment, you can flip me off again like you did the day after I brought you home again."

Justin curled into himself, scribbling on the paper. "This is stupid. You're acting like I'm... an idiot."

"Hey." He took Justin's chin and turned his head up so he could look into his lover's eyes. "I know I've talked to you before about BDSM. This is a part of it. The rules are there so you and I both know what's expected, so punishments and rewards happen. Sometimes just because that's what you want to have happen without expressly asking for it." He took a breath. "I would never, ever, believe you're an idiot or treat you like one."

"You promise? You don't think I'm... too stupid?" Justin was getting dangerously close to rule number one—no putting himself down, but Chris let it go because his boy needed the reassurance right now.

"I promise, Justin. You have to trust me—I have your best interests at heart and I think you're amazing and I love you." He drew Justin into his lap, lips near his boy's ear. "Besides, babe, think about how hot this is going to be. How much fabulous sex we're going to have."

Justin shivered, lips parting. He sucked on Justin's earlobe, pulling rhythmically. There, there that was better. This was about need, hunger, passion—about feeling.

"These here," he touched Justin's right nipple, then the left, giving each a pinch. "They should always be red, swollen, stunning. Make that a rule. Or put it as a part two of the no hiding them from me one."

"Don't." Justin pulled in, curling away.

"We still have to talk about punishments for not following the rules." He pinched a couple more times.

Justin shook his head, grabbed his wrists. "No punishments."

"Are you going to follow *all* the rules all the time, Justin?"

"I..." Justin's head shook.

"So we need punishments. And rewards. Just add no drinking and nips always to be beautiful and red, swollen to the list of rules first."

"No drinking?"

"I'll make exceptions sometimes, but no. No drinking."

"Why not? Nobody cares if I do. I don't drive when I'm buzzed." Justin scribbled on the paper, and Chris could see the outline of the man's hard prick in his shorts.

"Because you don't need to be buzzed on booze."

"I like drinking. I like how it numbs things."

"That's why you're not doing it anymore. I don't want things numb. I want you here and focused." He wanted his boy feeling everything, so in his own skin it was nearly unbearable. "Anything else we should add to the rule list before we talk about rewards and punishments?" He slid his hand down to cup Justin's ass, though he wanted that hard prick.

"I get to break the rules whenever I want?"

Oh, no. "Nice try, babe. But no."

"This whole thing..." Turned Justin on. Even if he wouldn't admit it.

"Is sexy. I know." Before Justin could even think to protest, Chris put his hand over that hard, needy prick.

"Hey." Justin rolled up, pushed into his touch.

How many things could they try? How far could they push together? He wrapped his fingers around Justin's heat. "So? No more rules for today?"

"What else do you want?"

"You'll have to take those cooking lessons. Supper will be your bailiwick, but I don't know if we need to make it a rule."

"I know how to order pizza."

Chris chuckled. "Man can not live on pizza alone." He wasn't sure Justin believed him. His boy would learn. He glanced at the list again. "Is there anything you want to see on the rules list?"

"Serious?" Justin looked at him, eyes suddenly young. "I want in the pool, every day."

If he hadn't been in love before, Chris would have been now. "Write it down. An hour of pool time every day."

"And you can't take it?"

He considered that and then nodded. "I can't take it. No punishment or test or anything will remove your hour of swimming. Nothing but, say, a freak blizzard or something unavoidable like that."

"Okay. Cool. That's what I want. I just... man, yesterday and today were so good."

"You looked amazing out there. Like you'd truly come home." And no way would he take that away from Justin. He'd do everything he could to make sure Justin got that hour every single day no matter what else was going on or happening. "Which brings us to rewards."

Justin actually relaxed against him. "That sounds fun."

He grinned. "That's the idea. You have any suggestions?"

"I want to hear yours."

"Off the top of my head... More pool time. Dinner ordered in instead of cooked by you. Blow job. Afternoon of movies."

"Dancing?"

Oh, that would be amazing. To dance with his boy. "Yes. Write them all down. Add massage, evening of rule

107

relaxation and hand jobs."

"Pancakes!" Justin laughed for him.

"I'm only putting them down if they're midnight pancakes." This was more fun than he'd thought it would be.

"I love midnight pancakes." Justin wrote them down, and added 'go to the beach'.

They were getting a great list going. "Like the rules list, this one can grow and change as we want."

Justin actually nodded for him.

"You ready for the last list, babe?"

"No."

That made him chuckle, squeeze his boy close. He tilted Justin's head and began kissing him again, hand fondling Justin's hard prick through his sweats. He wanted to know whether the punishments turned his boy on or not.

"Spanking always makes a good punishment." He whispered the words into Justin's ear.

"No spanking." That pretty cock lurched. Bingo.

"It's a punishment, babe. You're going to say no to all of them." He squeezed Justin's prick. "Put it on the list."

Justin's hand shook, but the word was scribbled down.

"What else..." Would Justin come up with any suggestions of his own?

"I don't know. I'm not good at this."

"Careful, Justin. No running yourself down."

"If it's true, then it's not running myself down."

"You haven't even tried, though. And who should know what a punishment for you would be better than you do?"

"I don't want to."

"Do it anyway. Just one. I can come up with the rest."

Justin was going to help him every evening, though, decide what punishments were deserved for the day, what rewards.

"I... You used to make me run laps?"

He nodded. "That works. We're going to be swimming every day anyway, so we can add going to the track on the days we need to."

He pointed to the paper and then tweaked one of Justin's nipples through his shirt. "Hiding these will get them clamped."

"No touching." Justin arched.

"That's not a rule. Write down the punishment on the list, babe."

"Uh-huh." Justin did it, grudgingly.

"What else..." He rubbed Justin's prick with one hand, the other pinching a pretty nipple.

"I don't know..." Justin curled away from him.

He tugged Justin back in. "We can start with the laps, the spanking and the nipple clamps and add things if we need to." He thought, maybe, his boy would respond best to punishments that fit the crime. "So, we start tomorrow. Do you want to go through punishments and rewards in the mornings or evenings?"

"Go through?"

"Yeah. I think it would benefit us if every morning, or every evening, we revisit the day and decide what punishments and what rewards are to be doled out."

"Night, I guess. I don't want to get in trouble. I don't know that I want to be in a place where I have to worry about that."

"Cool. We can have fun every evening going over our day." He kissed Justin's temple. "We'll start tomorrow."

Justin nodded, teeth worrying his bottom lip, digging in.

He reached out and put is finger on that abused lip, tugging it from Justin's teeth. "You have something you want to add?"

"No. I just. What about you? You have to have rules

too." Justin looked at him, so serious. "It's only fair."

"And what would you suggest?" This was a very interesting turn of events

"No random inventing rules and no slapping. No seeing other people and...we have to respect each other."

"No slapping?"

"No slapping." Justin looked very sure. "I won't let anyone slap my face. If you want to fight, we'll fight."

He blinked several times. It had never occurred to him to slap Justin. A low growl worked its way out of his throat. "Who slapped you?"

"I had a guy, back when we were swimming—one of the other guys. He did, when he was pissed. I hated it."

"Why didn't you tell me?" He wanted to wring the guy's neck and he didn't even know who it was. "Nobody touches my boy."

"I was scared. I was...hoping that he'd like me, I guess? I was young."

"I won't be slapping you. And neither will anyone else. I'm not interested in anyone else. And I do respect you. And new rules can be added during our discussion of the day, but not just whenever."

"Thank you." Justin leaned in, but the paper aside. "Can I just stay here a second?"

"Longer than a second. I'm hoping for a quickie before the food gets here."

Justin chuckled, stayed close, obviously needing him, comfort. He ran his hand along Justin's back, running his fingers up under Justin's t-shirt.

"Coach." Justin's head rested on his shoulder

"Yeah, babe?" He pulled his hands around to tweak Justin's beautiful little nips.

"Hey!" Justin pressed their chests together.

"I love your nips. I love playing with them." He pushed his hand between them and pinched again.

"They ache." Justin bit his shoulder.

"Good." He bit back, teeth worrying the skin of Justin's neck.

Justin jerked against him, cock still so hard in the soft shorts.

"Fuck, you're delicious." He hummed. "Take your shirt off for me. Lean back and show me your nipples."

He wanted Justin to ask for it. To ask for more.

"What?" Justin's was in constant motion, sliding on his thighs.

"I *know* you heard me."

"Yeah, but..."

"No, we'll get to your butt later." He couldn't resist the gentle tease. "For now, just take your shirt off and show me those nipples."

"They look just like they did earlier." The shirt came off, the broad chest with its sprinkling of hair exposed.

"I like looking at them. You're a sexy man, Justin." He reached out and flicked one of the little bits of flesh.

Justin tried to curl away, but he stopped the motion, arching Justin more. He licked his lips, the urge to worry those sweet tits with his teeth undeniable. Leaning in, he attacked the right one first. He bit it, then began sucking hard.

"Fuck..." Justin's voice was rough.

Chris rolled the tight nipple in between his teeth, pulled. Slapping it with his tongue, he nibbled the base before dragging his teeth up the tiny hard point. Justin cried out, ass rocking hard on his thighs. He needed to plug that sweet hole, let Justin's rocking do some extra work. A nice medium sized plug, one that would work the man's gland.

He let go of Justin's nipple, and looked into his boy's face. "I want you to go into the bedroom and the second drawer from the bottom has some toys. I want you to bring me a plug and the lube."

Justin's eyes went huge, wide.

He tapped Justin's ass lightly. "Now, babe."

"There's food coming."

"And I'll get the door when it comes. I think you'll find the plug will enhance your dining experience." It was going to enhance everything.

Justin looked at him, for a long second, then disappeared.

Which plug would Justin bring back with him? The smallest of them? The largest?

"Jesus Christ! How many pervy things do you have?"

He put his head back and laughed. "A few. We'll have to go shopping together one day soon."

"You know... that's probably illegal. I mean, there's stuff in this drawer that is insane!" Good thing he wasn't close to his neighbors, the way Justin was yelling.

"Bring out the most insane item along with the plug." He'd believed in the pit of his belly that his sub would come—his lover, his partner—and he'd prepared, gotten the things he wanted to try. And now they'd begin together. He couldn't wait to see what Justin brought him.

One of the plugs that looked like a three scoop ice cream was tossed in his lap, along with his box of medical sounds. "I mean, needles? Who are you poking? Who have you put those in? And the plugs? Are they clean?"

He wasn't going to crack up. He wasn't.

"Of course they're clean. I clean them even if they're right out of the box. And these aren't needles, babe." He opened the box and took out one of the thinner sounds. "Though they do go into your body."

"They don't go into *my* body." Justin stayed out of reach.

"They will." He made a 'come here' motion with his hand. "Come sit. You did bring the slick, right?"

"Uh-huh." Justin didn't move closer, though.

"Then come here. I won't bite, babe. At least not *that* hard."

Justin came to him, all nerves and need. He grabbed Justin's hair and tugged him down for a hard kiss. The cry was sweet, his boy's hands on his chest better.

He pulled Justin right down. The sounds could wait, but he wanted that ass plugged before their food arrived. He managed to get Justin face-down, over his lap. Oh, fuck. How hot was that? It was easy enough from there to tug the shorts down below Justin's ass. He rubbed the plug over it, slid it along Justin's crack.

"Coach?"

"Yeah, Justin?" He opened the bottle of slick.

"I want up."

Oh, not yet. "Once the plug is in." He put the latex on Justin's back and rubbed his slick fingers along the hot crack.

Justin's ass clenched, trying to keep him out.

"This'll be good, babe, I promise." He kept teasing his finger along the same path.

"I..." If Justin hadn't wanted this, he would have chosen a small one.

"It's me. Let me in."

"It's you." Justin took a deep, deep breath, then sighed, relaxed down.

"That's it, babe." He stroked over Justin's hole a few times and then gently pushed a single finger into the tight heat.

Justin moaned, shifted on his lap.

"Food will be a whole new experience with the plug inside you." He fucked Justin with just the one finger.

"In me? For how long?"

"At least as long as it takes us to eat." Though really, wasn't plugged how every day should start?

He'd love to watch Justin in the pool, full, stroking. Groaning, he pushed a second finger in with the first. Justin's grunt was delicious, as was the way his boy arched up, pressed back against him. He pushed his fingers in deep, searching out Justin's gland. Justin's ass clenched, rippled around his fingers and a sharp cry sounded as he found the flat gland.

"There we go." He kept touching that little spot deep inside Justin.

"Oh, God..." Justin's hands wrapped around his leg, body beginning to soften, open, need him.

"Yes." He pressed another finger in, using three now to open Justin up.

He could see the reaction all over his swimmer's skin. Stunning. His boy was stunning. He spread his fingers wide, stretching.

"Coach!" Justin's thighs spread.

"Right here, babe. Right here." He hit Justin's gland again.

Someone wasn't worrying about the plug or the rules or the food anymore. He fingerfucked Justin for a while, giving his boy as much pleasure as he could. Justin moaned, hips shuddering, shaking, cock driving down against him.

He grabbed the plug and managed to lube it one-handed. The first section would go in easy. He let his fingers slide away and pressed the head of the plug against Justin's hole. "Just let it happen."

"Please."

He didn't think Justin even knew what he was begging for.

He pushed gently, let that round head stretch Justin. Justin cried out, jerked, took more in. Moaning, he kept pushing. The tiny ring stretched for him. He pushed in harder, filling that beautiful ass. The widest part went in and then the little hole squeezed. Only two to go.

He lubed the next ball up and began to push again. His free hand drew little circles in the small of Justin's back.

"It's big." And Justin would take it, every inch.

"It'll fit. It'll fit perfectly." He shoved the second segment in. One left, this one bigger.

"Is it in?'

"One more segment to go, babe. You're doing great."

"It won't fit."

"Trust me, it will."

"You're sure?" Justin was rocking, pushing back into his touch.

"I'm sure." He let Justin's own movements take the rest of the plug in.

When the widest part of the plug spread Justin, his boy bucked, hand pushing between them.

"What are you doing?" Chris grabbed Justin's hand, keeping him from touching himself.

"It's caught. I'm hard. Fuck."

"Easy. I know you're hard. We'll deal with that once this is properly seated."

"I'm caught in my shorts."

"Just relax and let me finish this." He pushed the plug the rest of the way in, Justin's body almost snapping around the base.

Justin cried out, rolling off his lap, landing hands and knees on the floor.

"Hey, hey." He put his hands on Justin, easing his boy. "Careful. You have to trust me."

Justin leaned up into his lap. "It's big."

"You chose it, babe." He helped Justin untangle himself from his shorts.

"I didn't know."

"It was the one that drew you." He helped Justin to

sit next to him, knowing that plug was shifting inside his boy with the slightest movements.

Justin tried to stand.

"No, you can stay with me." He let his hand brush the hard, needy prick.

Justin shook, arched into his touch.

He wrapped his hand around Justin's cock and moved slowly. "No? You don't want this?"

"I..." Justin groaned, legs spreading.

"I've got you, babe. That's all that matters." He kept moving slowly, not wanting Justin to tip over too quickly—let that sweet ass work the plug, feel how good it was to have inside.

If he timed it right, he could keep Justin needing, aroused, all through supper, then let Justin explode.

The doorbell rang and he let go of Justin's prick, setting his boy next to him. "Don't move and don't you dare touch yourself."

"Don't let them see me?"

"They can't from the door, I promise."

He kissed the side of Justin's mouth and went to the door, paying for their feast, giving the guy a good tip. It wasn't long at all before he was coming back into the living room. Justin was curled on the sofa, leaning on one hip.

Chris stopped for a moment, cock jerking in his sweats. "Damn, babe, you're gorgeous."

Those pretty eyes stared at him, needy, wanting.

He put the food down on the coffee table and grabbed Justin's discarded t-shirt, placing it over his babe's lap. "I don't want you burning anything important."

"No burning." Justin was breathing hard.

"No, that would be bad." He started taking stuff out of the take-out bag.

Justin shivered. "I don't know if I can eat."

"It should make everything taste even better. All your senses are on alert."

"Have you done it before?"

He couldn't help but tease. "Eaten Chinese food?"

"Butthead." Justin stuck his tongue out.

Chris laughed and settled with Justin. He grabbed a pair of chopsticks and opened up the sesame chicken. He knew it was Justin's favorite. Justin licked his lips, actually moved closer. He snagged a piece of the chicken and held it up to Justin's lips.

Justin opened for him, ate the bite. "Thank you."

"You're welcome. How does it stack up?"

"It's cool. Salty. Spicy."

"Good." He found the egg rolls. "Here they are."

Justin took one, nibbled it, oh so carefully. He grabbed another and ate it far less daintily, moaning happily when it proved to be pretty damn good. Crispy on the outside, hot and tasty on the inside. He dipped the second one in the plum sauce and that made it even better.

But best of all was watching Justin eat, knowing his plug was filling Justin up. So careful not to move his hips, every movement Justin made was planned, delicious.

When Justin had polished off the egg roll, Chris handed over a pair of chopsticks. "You choose next." It would force Justin to move, to feel the plug shifting inside him.

Justin looked panicked—utterly and totally panicked.

"I... You. It." Justin took a deep breath. "It's *in* me, man."

"I know." He soothed a hand along Justin's arm. "It's going to move inside you as you move, make everything just light up."

Justin leaned hard, rested into his hand.

"This is a good thing, babe. Not a punishment."

"It's big." Justin rolled over, moaning as he reached for another box.

"Tell me what it feels like."

"It's moving in me, stretching me."

"It's lighting you up from the inside out." Because he knew the feelings were in more than just Justin's ass. Justin nodded, almost moving into his lap. He let Justin stay close, and nodded at the array of food on the coffee table. "So what are you picking?"

"I don't care." Justin rubbed against him, grabbed a box.

Laughing softly, Chris let his hand slip beneath Justin's t-shirt to touch that needy prick for a quick moment.

The box dropped to the coffee table, Justin pushing into his touch. "Please."

"We need to eat first, babe." He let go of Justin's prick, petting the sweet belly instead.

"Chris. Coach." Justin groaned for him, arched.

He kissed Justin softly, unable to resist.

"Please, Coach..." Sweet, needy boy.

"I want you to feed me first." He slid his hand around to Justin's back, gently kneading the little knot of nerves at the base of Justin's spine.

"I ache..." Justin began to relax for him, though, hum.

"I know. Learn to savor that feeling. There's nothing wrong in delaying gratification."

"Savor it? Like it's good."

"Isn't it?"

"I don't know!" Frustrated lover.

"I think it's good." He licked the corner of Justin's mouth. "I'm hungry, babe. Feed me."

Justin took another, hard, hungry kiss.

He pulled back, smiling. "Now with food."

"Okay." Justin was clumsy, fingers trembling, but his boy fed him a bite.

He hummed softly over the crispy beef. It was very good and he opened his mouth, silently asking for another piece. Justin was steadier for this bite.

"Find us something we haven't tried yet." Justin would have to move for that.

"Oh. I." Justin shifted, then stopped, shaking hard.

"You're doing great, babe."

His fingers were squeezed, then Justin grabbed some fried rice. "I can't feed you rice with the chop sticks."

"Then pick something else."

"You want another egg roll?"

"I'd love another egg roll."

"Thank god." Those words were whispered, Justin reaching for the open box.

He laughed softly, nudged Justin so he shifted on the couch.

"Coach!" Justin arched a little, cock bobbing.

"Yeah, babe?" He nudged Justin over again.

"Don't. Fuck." Justin stood, licking his lips over and over.

He let his eyebrow go up. If Justin took even a single step, he'd move that plug far more than just shifting in his seat could cause.

"Help me?"

Leaning in, he wrapped his lips around Justin's prick, sucking it in.

"Coach!" Justin jerked, hips pushing deep, the sound utterly shocked.

He would have grinned, but his mouth was full, so instead he simply tugged, sucking on the sweet, needy flesh.

"Oh. Oh, fuck. Please. Please." Justin's hand landed on his head.

He took his time, sucking and licking, head bobbing slowly on the hard flesh. Reaching around Justin, he tapped the base of the plug.

"God..." Justin went stiff, up on tiptoe.

He tapped the base of the plug again, slapping the tip of Justin's cock with his tongue at the same time. His boy came hard, sobbing out his name. He swallowed Justin down, still pulling hard on the long prick, making sure Justin had plenty of aftershocks to shudder and shiver through.

"Coach..." His boy was about to lose it, voice overwhelmed, shocked.

He licked and sucked and finally let Justin's prick slide from his lips. Justin pushed into his arms, wrapped around him and held on.

"I've got you, babe. I've got you." He stroked Justin's back.

Justin nodded, squeezed him, shaking in his arms.

"You've never come so hard before, have you?"

Justin shook his head, face hidden in his neck.

"It's going to be good like that a lot, babe. I can promise you that." He was planning to blow Justin's mind on a regular basis. And he would be there for comfort, support, love after, every time.

He kissed the top of Justin's head and hummed softly, rocking his lover.

Eventually they'd settle together. Finish eating. Breathe. But for now he held his lover, his boy. His Justin.

Chapter Nine

Justin woke up to the scent of coffee, and he got up, and started moving, stumbling into the shower, totally on autopilot.

He was standing under the hot spray when the shower curtain was pushed to the side. "How about some company?"

"Coach." He blinked, grinning. It didn't seem real sometimes.

"That's me." Coach grinned and stepped up behind him.

Justin leaned back, snuggled right in. "Morning."

"Morning, babe." Coach's kiss landed on his shoulder, noisy and slightly open-mouthed.

Justin chuckled, stretching under the water. Coach's fingers slid over him, tracing the muscles of his chest, his belly. That touch made his abs jerk, roll.

"Mmm. God, you're sexy," Coach murmured against his skin.

"Too early to be sexy."

Coach chuckled. "Never too early for that. In fact, bed-rumpled Justin is one of my favorite variations."

The words made him smile, let him lean harder. Coach hummed for him, fingers continuing to travel over his body. The water was warm, Coach's fingers were warmer. They slid toward his prick and then away, moving around to cup his ass cheeks. Thank god Chris had taken the plug out last night. His hole felt sensitive, a little swollen—not like his nipples, God, but good.

Coach pressed a thumb against it and rubbed, but didn't try to push in. His body clenched, rippled, and he moaned.

"Sweet, sensitive hole." Coach bit at his shoulder, teeth scraping on his skin.

"Uh-huh..." Justin groaned, skin just too small.

"You taste like mine," muttered Coach, mouth wrapping around his skin and sucking where those teeth had scraped.

What did that mean? He spread, his hips rocking back.

"Mmm. Needy." Coach's fingers slid over his belly again but instead of moving down to grab his cock, they slid up toward his nipples. He shook his head, going up on tiptoe. "You can't hide them from me. It's a rule." Coach rubbed his nipples, almost gently, lulling him before pinching them hard.

"Coach!" He pulled away, slip-sliding a second.

Catching him, Coach pulled him back against the solid body. "Careful, J."

"I. I'm going for a run."

He wanted some time alone.

"Are you trying to hide from me?"

"Yes." He didn't like that. Having Chris make him think the touch was sweet and then hurting.

"Why?"

"Because I didn't like that. If you're going to love on me, don't make the peace disappear on me."

"I was loving on you." Chris sounded confused.

"I know, and you made me relax and then you pinched me. That's mean."

"I didn't do it to be mean."

He searched Chris' eyes. "It felt mean."

"It wasn't mean, babe. I wanted to make you spark."

"I don't spark in the morning. You know that." He was... slow to wake, at best.

"That wasn't true yesterday, or the day before." Well, yeah, Coach had woken him with orgasms.

"But you were..." God, sometimes he was just stupid. "Whatever." He wasn't going to worry about it.

"I'll make a new rule. No pinching in the mornings. But, we still make them swollen in the mornings."

He looked at Chris. "Okay. Okay." Something tight and unhappy inside him eased and he pushed into Chris' arms.

Chris turned his face up and kissed him, tongue pushing into his mouth. Justin opened, kissed Chris back, relaxing, letting himself feel it.

Their tongues tangled for a while, and then Chris began to kiss his way down toward Justin's nipples. Chris had promised not to pinch, and Justin believed him. Trusted, so he arched, let Coach in. Chris slapped his tongue against one nipple, fingers playing gently with the other. Then Coach began to suck. Justin whimpered, the suction so soft, but huge somehow, vast, pulling at him.

Coach's hands wrapped around his waist, pulling their hips together, their pricks bumping, rubbing so nicely. The pressure became an ache, and he moaned, his balls so heavy. His nipple was given a last lick, then Coach moved over to the other one. The water pouring on his right nipple ached and he sucked in a sobbing breath.

Without warning, Coach let go of his nipple and bent double, mouth wrapping around his prick.

"Coach!" He never would have guessed his Coach would be so... oral.

Coach just pulled harder, hands creeping back up his chest to his nipples.

"Gonna." He slid his hands down Chris' arms.

Golden

That had Chris increasing his suction. Justin grunted, went up on tiptoe, and shot, shaking through it. Chris kept sucking for a few minutes and then let him slide from that hot mouth. He slumped back against the tile, staring, dazed.

Chris kissed his way upward, stopping to lap and lick and suck at his nipples, making them ache and ache. It felt so good, though, and he let himself breathe through it. Coach hummed, hand stroking his belly and it felt like being praised. Justin moaned, fingers stuttering through Chris' wet hair.

His nipple was pulled away from his chest, his skin stretched, and then Chris let it go and brought their mouths together for a kiss. He pushed into the touch, hoping that Chris was needing him, wanting. Groaning, Chris pushed back, prick thick, hot against his belly.

"What do you want?" he asked, ready to give Chris anything.

"You, babe."

The words made him moan, deepen the kiss with a cry. Chris grabbed his right leg and tugged it up over Chris' hip. He nodded, pushed close, hands on Chris' shoulder.

"Come on up," murmured Coach, taking his other leg and encouraging him up.

"Am I too heavy?"

"Fuck no, come on, roll up so I can get in."

He tried to move, to make his body do what Chris said.

Chris' hands were on his ass, tilting him and then that hard, hot prick was right there, pressing against him. "Babe, you're clean, yeah?"

"I've never, not with anyone but you."

"I'm clean. And I would never risk hurting you." Coach pushed, prick nudging against his hole.

No. No, Chris wouldn't. Coach cared for him.

124

That thick prick pushed in, spreading him slowly. Coach's eyes were huge, the look of shocked pleasure delicious. "Fuck. Justin. Oh, God." The words slid into moans.

"Good?"

"Fuck yes. Never done it bareback before."

Neither had he, but Coach knew that

"Hot. Fuck, Justin." Coach leaned their foreheads together and looked into his eyes as the thick cock pushed deep inside him.

Justin inhaled, holding the gaze, drowning in it.

Once Coach was seated all the way in, Justin's back up against the tile, Coach began to pull out again. He felt every single inch, deep inside him, heavy. Coming almost all the way out, Coach then pushed back in, nudging his gland on the way. That made his stomach tighten, jerk as pleasure lit him up. Moaning, Coach repeated the move, making it happen again. He wasn't hard again, but that didn't mean he couldn't go with it, ride it. Coach's face was amazing to watch, pleasure etching deeper with each movements.

"You look so happy." He loved that look on Chris' face.

"Make me happy. You do, I mean."

"Good." The words were fierce, even to his own ears.

Coach smiled at him, thrust in harder, faster. They found a rhythm like running, one they could keep up for hours. Chris' lips touch his again and again, tongue sliding, sipping almost from his mouth. Their bellies slid together, slick from the water and their sweat, because they were both working hard.

"So hot, babe." Chris panted, the words almost whispers lost beneath the sound of the water.

"Uh-huh. Burning."

Chris moved faster, thrusting into him. He groaned,

belly tight, driving back, the pressure inside him huge. One of Chris' hands slipped between them, wrapping around his cock.

"I can't. Not again. Just focus on you."

"Shh." Chris matched his pulls to his thrusts.

His lips opened, and he fought to pull in air. Chris' mouth found the join where his shoulder met his neck and began to work up a mark, sucking softly.

"Oh, fuck..." The gentle touch made his entire body ripple.

Coach hummed, kept sucking, kept thrusting, kept pulling, all the sensations meeting in the middle somehow. Caught between boneless and having jerking, rippling muscles, Justin just flew. Chris moved faster and faster,

"Coach." He couldn't believe it, but he was going to go. Again.

"Together this time, babe."

"Uh-huh. Together." He didn't bother to argue.

"Right now." Chris squeezed the head of his prick even as that hard cock inside him slammed deep and Chris froze.

The orgasm left him shaken, sucking in near-hysterical breaths. Chris held him against the tile, murmuring softly into his neck as the water came down around them. The arms around him were the only things that held him together.

"Love you, babe," murmured Chris.

Justin kissed Chris' shoulder.

"All days should start like this." Listen to the satisfaction in Chris' voice.

Justin chuckled, the sound rough, husky.

"You don't agree?"

"I'm melted. Bone deep." Like utterly.

"Perfect."

Chris kissed him, hard and quick, and then carefully let

him down. His legs barely held him, his knees buckling.

"I've got you," Chris assured him, arm around him as the water was turned off.

"Sorry. You make me dizzy." He grabbed towels.

"I like that."

He handed Coach a towel, wrapped one around himself. Coach pulled him in close and kissed him again, tongue sliding lazily through his mouth. God, he could go back to bed, sleep for a week.

"You want to go to breakfast, babe?"

"I could totally eat." He nuzzled Chris' jaw, hummed.

"Me, too. A nice big plate of eggs and bacon and sausage and home fries, toast...."

"Gonna make me fat." They both chuckled at that. He had an amazing metabolism. It took mass quantities of food to keep him going.

"I'll make you swim extra laps if that looks like it's going to happen." Coach hauled him in for another kiss, one that left him breathless and reminded him he'd just been fucked into bonelessness.

How did Coach *do* that?

Grabbing him around his waist, Coach lifted his feet off the ground and walked him back into the bedroom. His laugh rang out, and he shook his head. Crazy man.

Coach carried him right to the bed, laying him down on the mattress. "Laughing at me..."

"At us." He curled up in the covers.

Coach joined him. "I thought we were going to go feed your bottomless pit."

"Mmmhmm." Food. Yum, but... warm blankets...

Coach laughed softly, and blew air against his belly. "I'll just have to eat you up."

"Coach!" He loved how Chris made him smile.

The blowing continued, moving to his hip, and then over his prick.

"Tickles. Tickles, Coach."

Chris just chuckled and blew against his balls. That didn't tickle. That felt good, and his legs drew up. Chris' hum also felt good, vibrating through him. The soft touch of air to him left him with goose pimples. That was oddly intimate—not arousing, he was too sated for that—but it warmed him, deep inside. The soft touches and kisses and blows of air continued, Chris touching the skin behind his balls, blowing on his hole, nuzzling his inner thighs.

"You... That's my hole, Coach."

Coach's head popped up, looked at him, eyes mock-wide. "It is?"

"Yes." He snorted, grinned.

Chris grinned up at him, licked his hole and gave him a wink.

"Hey..." He pulled away, sighed.

Coach frowned. "What's wrong?"

"Nothing. Nothing, I just... I can't get it up again."

"So?"

Justin shrugged. "I... You licked me."

"I'm enjoying you. It doesn't have to lead to anything." Coach stroked his inner thighs.

He'd never had anyone touch him without wanting something.

Soft kisses followed Coach's fingers, then he rubbed his cheek along the same path. Justin couldn't decide whether he wanted to pull away, push closer. The gentle touches were unnerving as fuck.

"You smell so good down here." Coach nosed his balls and rubbed the patch of skin behind them.

"You... you can't say things like that..." Could he?

"Why not? It's the truth." He could feel Coach, breathing in deeply.

"Because it's..." Justin didn't even know. He didn't have an answer.

"Sexy?" Coach grinned at him.

"It's just... people don't say things like that."

"I'm not people, babe."

His right ball was tugged into Chris' mouth. The heat surrounded him, and he groaned—less turned on than melty, weirdly soothed. Chris hummed, then let his ball go, took in the other one. It was like being covered with a heated blanket, making his limbs feel heavy.

When Chris was done, he kissed his way up Justin's body, ending with his mouth for a long, slow kiss. Justin felt loved. Adored. Like he was home.

Coach curled up around him, settling in with him like there was nothing better to do all day than be together like this. He rested down, took a deep breath. He could handle this. He so could.

"Love you, Justin."

He kissed Coach's chest. Good. This was good.

Chapter Ten

Chris watched the kids swimming up and down the lanes. Okay, he watched Justin watching the kids swim. Once they'd each done twenty laps, he was going to introduce them to Justin, let the kids do a little hero-worship. The kids and Justin both deserved it. But in the meantime, he was watching his lover's face.

Justin was hungry for it. Those eyes were looking at the water like he was watching his competition, not his students. Justin would have already done his laps, except they'd... uh, 'slept in' and now Justin was going to have to wait until after the practice for his daily swim.

Besides, Chris wasn't sure if he'd have gotten to see this hungry side of Justin if he'd already had his swim and Chris needed to see it. It confirmed what he was beginning to suspect—retired or not, Justin wasn't done competing. Justin had work to do—a lot of it—but the chops were still there, the basics.

He wandered over. "So? What do you think?"

"About what?"

"About the kids. See any potential here?" He was pretty sure Justin would make a great assistant coach; Justin knew what it took, what a good swimmer looked like, after all.

"Couple of them. Lane three. Six."

Chris nodded and grinned. Bang on. He'd known

Justin could do the coaching thing. He was pretty sure, though, that it would be a few more years before Justin had time to help him coach. Four in fact—there were more gold medals in his swimmer. Justin wasn't done. Oh, he'd needed the break when he'd left; Chris was sure that had been the right thing, but he could read the hunger in Justin, even if his boy didn't know it was there yet. He thought Justin needed to prove it to himself as much as anything.

"Yeah, that's my thought, too. I'm not sure lane three has the dedication, though." Maybe if Justin talked to them. Hell, maybe if Justin trained with them...

"He either does or he doesn't. You can't make that."

"You can find the right carrot, though. Not everyone is a natural like you." The swimming itself was all the carrot Justin had ever needed. It was what made him special.

"What do you use?" Justin was pacing, watching

"I'm wondering if meeting a gold-medalist and dangling the Olympics in front of him will help Daniel. Jessica, though, she's lane six. I think she's hungry for it all on her own."

"She's strong. Confident. Are they old enough to be in the gym?"

"I have to clear it with their folks, but yeah, if you agree on their talent, I'd like to talk to them about going to the next level."

"Maybe six. I don't like the idea of carrots." Or maybe Justin just didn't want to be the carrot.

"You ready to meet them? And then you can show them how it's really done."

"Okay. Sure. I like kids, you know that." Back in their heyday, Justin had mentored a lot of children, young swimmers.

"I know, babe." It was one of the reasons why he

thought Justin would make a great assistant coach.

"You better not call me that at work, you'll get in trouble."

He nodded; it had just slipped out. "I'm not hiding you, though."

"You have to, don't you?"

"If someone fires me for being gay they'll have a lawsuit against them." Of course if Justin went back into the sport, he might not want the world to know he was fucking his coach.

"Good to know." Justin actually grinned. "They're on lap eighteen."

"Then I guess we better rescue 'em, huh?" He gave Justin a wink and raised his whistle to his mouth.

Justin went to the wall, leaned, eyes on the water. Chris gave five sharp whistles, his swimmers coming to a stop when they hit the wall. He heard Justin's soft, husky laugh. His lips twisted; Justin knew his whistle well.

He headed for the kids. "Hey, guys, I have a treat for you today. This is Justin Pattern, four-time Olympic Gold medal champion."

The kids stopped, stared, then the squealing and yammering started.

"Oh, my god. Was he watching us? Did he see us swim?"

He chuckled. "You can talk to him directly—he doesn't bite." At least Justin hadn't yet.

"Are you sure? He's really tall."

He grinned over at Justin. "Sit down, J."

"Sure, Coach." Justin pulled up a chair, plopped down. "Hey, guys. So you want to be swimmers?"

Chris grinned and sat on one of the bleachers, watching the kids and Justin interact. Justin was easy, laughing, relaxed with the kids. Fuck, Chris loved this man. Totally and truly. He would do everything in his power to make sure Justin was happy and fulfilled and loving life.

He'd fucked up, completely, shutting Justin out. He'd almost lost the most wonderful thing that had ever happened to him, and for what? He'd thought it was for Justin's own good, to let Justin stand as his own man. Instead, it had clearly left his beautiful boy flailing. He'd spend the rest of his life making up for that mistake, making sure Justin knew he was talented, special, loved. His.

Justin met his eyes. "I don't know. I think he's a pretty good coach."

He gave Justin a grin. He'd been caught in his own head. "Only pretty good?" he asked.

"Yep. He used to be great, once upon a time." Oh, little shit.

He shook his head. "Time to get in the water, Justin. Do some work."

"Me?" Justin grinned, winked. "Do I remember how to swim?"

He winked right back. "I don't know. You used to be great. Once upon a time."

"Yep. Long time ago. What lane?"

"Four of course."

Brat. God, Chris loved him.

Justin stood up, stripped off his sweats. The kids were staring, open-mouthed. They were going to get quite a show; his boy had been the best, and was still fucking good.

Justin looked at him. "What are we swimming?"

"Give me two hundred of each."

Let the kids see how fast Justin was, how each stroke was supposed to look. Even out of practice, he'd seen better form from Justin the last couple days than he'd seen from any of the kids.

"No problem." Justin cut into the water and started

moving, body working like a machine.

"You guys watching? Pretty cool, huh?" It always caught his full attention when Justin started swimming.

Half the kids were just fascinated, a few unimpressed, but a couple of them? They were hungry for it. The two that Justin had pointed out, in fact. Chris nodded, pleased.

His swimmer moved fast, then Jessica joined him. She couldn't keep up, but the girl was seriously trying.

That was their up and coming swimmer. She really would do well with Justin in the pool with her. Chris could imagine sending them both to the 2016 Olympics.... and Jessica was young enough to go through '24...

He could feel that old excitement starting at the base of his spine again. The one he always felt with Justin, but a little sharper now, a little more. Two swimmers. He could have two swimmers at the next Olympics and then Jessica for the next two after that, maybe another swimmer or two from the next crop of kids. He and Justin could have quite the stable...

Oh, fuck, he was making some long term plans in his head. He had done this with Justin, years ago, and it had worked, mostly. Right up until he'd let Justin retire and had kicked Justin out of the proverbial nest to help him fly on his own.

Okay. Enough kicking himself in the ass over that one; he needed to move forward.

He cheered Jessica and Justin on, and nodded at the other kids. "Don't you want to go up against a champion?"

A number of them shook their heads, obviously intimidated.

"Justin would love to have you in the pool with him."

Daniel started swimming, one of the other girls—Jessica's best friend, not very good at swimming, but very good at trying.

"That's it! If you want it, you have to take it, guys. No one is going to hand out medals because you'd like to have one."

Slowly, all the others joined in. Jessica was struggling—they'd all already done laps and she was reaching muscle failure.

He blew his whistle as she got near the wall, calling them all out of the pool He didn't want to dampen her enthusiasm and there was no reason she had to keep up with Justin. Yet.

Justin kept swimming, letting him talk them down, point out Justin's form. They spent another fifteen minutes there, and then he dismissed them for the day, promising to bring Justin back tomorrow.

Justin kept swimming, taking one lap after another. Chris let him, sitting on the edge of the pool and kicking his feet.

Finally the blond head popped up. "So, did they like it?"

"You're their rock star, J."

"Used to be."

"Uh-huh." He could see the way Justin was glowing from the day.

"Gonna do a few more. Just to feel them."

Chris chuckled. That's why Justin was a champion. "I'll swim with you, babe."

"Cool." Justin took off, not worrying about him in the least.

He didn't mind. He wasn't going to try to keep up with Justin, but he enjoyed being in the pool with his swimmer; he had to work out to keep in shape, so it might as well be in the pool. Justin wasn't a sprinter, he was in for the long races, body meant to conserve energy. Justin didn't do badly in the 400s, but it was the 800 and the 1500 where he excelled, where Justin had won his gold medals.

Chris still couldn't keep up with him for more than a lap or two and so he didn't try. It felt good to be in the water, though, to know that Justin was the person sharing the pool with him. To know that his swimmer, his boy, was in the water again.

He did half a dozen laps and then rolled to his back to crawl lazily up and down until Justin was ready to come out. The swimming went for almost another hour before he went for the whistle. He thought maybe Justin would have swum all day if he'd let him.

He found enough breath to blow three times, and then sat at the edge of the pool, panting.

Justin pushed it, doing an extra lap before slowing down.

"You need to listen to and obey the whistles, J." He wagged his finger, but despite the joking gesture, he was serious.

Justin rolled his eyes, but nodded. "I was going to."

How many times had he heard that? He shook his head. "Going to schmoe-ing to—you *do*. That's an order."

Justin treaded water, moving slow. "So, what now?"

"You need to eat. We can talk about how you want to proceed while we do."

"Proceed?" Justin moved to the edge, slowly.

"With coaching, with swimming. You're looking pretty damn good out there."

"Thanks." Justin pulled himself up. "You think your bosses will be okay with me working here?"

"Yeah, I do. Jessica's parents especially are going to be all for it because she is going to get home today and be glowing with enthusiasm."

"She's got something."

"She does. She jumped right into the pool with you, too. We can nurture that spark and get her to the 2016 Olympics, I'm sure of it. She'll be sixteen then, and I bet she makes the squad."

"Cool." Justin headed for the towels, dried off, then gathered the wet ones. "I'm assuming part of what I do is towels?"

"Yep. Low man on the totem pole, and all." He was going to like having an assistant. He would like having Justin as a swimmer even better.

Justin nodded, grabbed his phone, earphones. "So where's the laundry room?"

"Follow me." He wondered how long it would be before Justin started making competing again noises.

Chris gave him two months and if it hadn't happened by then, he'd put the seed into Justin's ear. Justin followed, one earphone in, mind somewhere else. Probably still in the pool.

He showed Justin where the laundry was and settled with one hip against the dryer. "So what do you think? Are you going to enjoy working with me?"

"Sure. I mean, it's a little sad, to be the towel guy, but at least I'm in the pool."

"You're more than the towel boy, and you know it. Towels are just one of the assistant coach's duties."

"I know." Justin chuckled and started the washer. "You know me, if I could just swim, I'd just swim."

"It's a shame you retired." He watched Justin closely as he said the words.

"I had to. I was getting older. I was tired. I didn't want to do it anymore and I..." Justin wouldn't meet his eyes. "I thought you and me could hook up. I wanted you so bad."

Regret lurched through him again at having pushed Justin out of the nest as fully and as hard as he had. "You never said anything."

"I was going to, but then... there wasn't a reason. I mean, you didn't want me, then."

"I was just fucking good at hiding it, J." He went over and put his hands on Justin's cheeks, made his boy look at him. "I've wanted you to be mine for a long time."

"I thought I was. I had this stupid idea that..." Justin rolled his eyes, shook his head.

"No. Tell me. I want to hear what you have to say."

"Well, I don't want to say it. Just let it go, man."

"Justin..." He growled a little.

"What?" Oh, pushing.

"Tell me. Or else." Chris could push, too.

"Or else what?"

"I'll have to spank you."

"I don't. This. We're at work!"

"We're the only ones here. And the rules still apply."

Justin tugged away from him, "Look, what's in my head doesn't belong to you. You only get to know what I want you to. You don't get to see my heart until I'm ready!"

"My heart is already yours, Justin. I don't want to waste anymore time worrying over what happened in the past. And I want all of you—the things you tell me and the things you don't want to tell me."

"Too bad. I'm keeping my stupidity to myself. Deal with it."

He growled at his boy. "You are not fucking stupid, boy and neither are your thoughts or emotions." That was one rule broken.

Justin glared. "It's none of your business. I had a stupid dream that you'd turn around in the hotel after I announced my retirement and tell me you'd just been waiting for me to do it, you'd just wanted to make sure everything was clear before you could kiss me." His lover snorted. "Instead you told me to make sure I started job hunting, that you needed my room. I was all used up, and it was time for you to find someone else to work with."

He'd never—not once—suggested Justin was worthless or used up. Not one time. "I did not say that. Yes, I wanted you to stand on your own. I wanted you to find your own way because I was not going to force myself on you. I was all you knew, how could I justify making a move on you? But I never, ever, not once said that you were either worthless or used up." He knew he was practically snarling the words, but he was pissed off, damn it!

"You didn't even care what the hell happened to me. All those years together and you never once even called me!"

"I didn't think I could! Not without begging you to come home to me. And that was clearly a mistake, one that I regret, but you can't keep punishing us both for it."

"Sure I can." Justin looked at him, looking ten years older, all of the sudden. "I shouldn't, because it's just stupid and won't help, but don't fool yourself. I totally can."

He wasn't going to let Justin do that. Growling, he grabbed Justin up and pressed a hard kiss on Justin's lips. Justin moaned and pushed into his arms, pouring all that energy into him, trusting him with it. Chris took the kiss deeper, letting Justin know that he was being claimed. Justin was his boy. Period, full stop.

And if Justin started swimming again, well, fuck everyone who had a problem with them. Lots of spouses coached their loved ones. He felt it when Justin relaxed, when his boy gave in and let him inside. He hummed his approval, hand finding Justin's ass and holding on.

He loved the hint of chlorine on Justin's lips. It felt so right, so how Justin should taste. Groaning, he pressed them closer together, fucking Justin's lips wildly. Justin's cock was hard, his boy humping, rubbing off against him.

Chris glanced at the door; good, they'd closed it and he'd locked it after coming in.

He encouraged Justin's movements. He shoved his hand in Justin's pants, into the still-wet suit. He found Justin's hard prick and wrapped his hand around it, the heat of it burning against his palm. Justin humped hard, driving, pushing him with needy little sounds. He rubbed his thumb across the tip; they never did go into what the sounds were, not properly but he wanted to fuck Justin's slit.

Justin cried out into his lips and came, heat spraying over his fingers.

"That's my boy."

"Oh, god. Chris." Justin moaned, kiss going sloppy.

He couldn't help but smile, which didn't help the kiss take shape any better, but he didn't care. He had his boy's softening prick in his hand, the smell of spunk mixing with chlorine and laundry soap, like the best cologne ever. He kept the kisses going, easing back, letting Justin breathe.

"Mine," he added. "All mine."

"Yeah. Yeah, man."

"You could say it with more conviction, because it's true."

"We just rubbed off at work. That's conviction."

He chuckled. "You got off. I'm still hard."

"You need to catch up." Justin winked at him, playful, teasing.

"You going to help me with that?" He took Justin's hand and placed it on his crotch.

"I am. We won't get in trouble, right? I don't want to fuck up your job."

"Door's locked, babe." He put his hands on Justin's shoulders, encouraging him down.

Justin knelt, moving easily. Sweet hungry little cockhound. He didn't undo his swimming trunks, letting Justin work for his prick Justin tugged the hair above his cock, pulling the suit down. He grunted, slid his hand through Justin's hair.

"Sorry, Coach." Justin's warm lips nuzzled his pubes.

"S'okay—you surprised me." He kept stroking Justin's hair, groaning as Justin's chin brushed the base of his cock.

"Horny man." Justin dragged his tongue along the shaft, then set to sucking him off.

He was going to reply, but the suction was too fucking good and he let it go, focused on his boy and the things Justin was doing to him. Steady and strong, Justin sucked like a Hoover, pulling him in, swallowing around him.

"Oh, fuck, babe. Not a race." He wasn't really complaining, though. Justin was going to make him come, make him lose it. "Soon." The word was more of a moan, but it was the best warning he could manage with the way Justin was lighting up his prick.

Justin groaned, rolling his balls, pushing him.

"Eager boy." He tightened his hands in Justin's hair and moaned.

Justin's answer was to take him in, swallow around his cock. His hips bucked, pushing his cock even deeper as he came down his boy's throat. Justin didn't lose a drop. Not one drop.

He kept hold of Justin's head long after his boy had cleaned him and let him slip from between those lips.

"We should go to work. You're going to get in trouble." Justin kissed his belly.

"We have kids at four o'clock, but we're free until then."

"Still." Stubborn man.

"Put my prick away and we'll go have some lunch. You can work up a schedule for the kids—I want to see how you think they should be training based on what you saw today."

"Okay, okay." Justin tucked him in, stood, straightening his clothes.

He stroked Justin's cheek and pulled him in close for another kiss. "We also need to see about cooking classes and start getting organized on grocery shopping and shit."

"You're serious about that?"

"You know I am—we made it a rule, didn't we?"

"Yeah, but... I don't cook, man."

"Hence the cooking classes."

Really, two grown men couldn't go their whole lives without ever using the kitchen except for the very basics. Justin rolled his eyes, but they headed out, leaving the grinding of the washing machine behind. They'd change the towels over when they got back.

"What do you feel like for lunch?"

"I'm easy. Pizza?"

Christ. He was going to outlaw pizza. "How are you not sick to death of pizza? You can have anything you want, the sky's the limit. Pick something other than pizza."

"Uh. Turkey sandwiches."

"Subway it is." He got into the car, grinning over at Justin. "Thanksgiving this year, we'll make our own turkey, and have leftover sandwiches for a week."

Justin looked at him, obviously surprised. "We will? I... Okay. Okay. I'd like that. You know my folks—they don't cook."

No. No, Justin's people were unique, to say the least. Two incredibly intellectual people who had two incredibly physical children. Justin's sister had been one hell of a distance runner, but she'd died at twenty, just keeled over from a heart condition.

"A turkey and all the fixings. Even if it kills us. So we'd better get you signed up for those cooking classes soon." They'd be in trouble if at least one of them didn't have a decent grasp of the basics by the time November rolled around.

"Us. I'm not taking them alone."

He supposed it wouldn't hurt to learn. "Suppers are going to be your job, though."

"Why? Why do you want me to cook?"

"You'll be setting the menus, making your shopping list. I'll go shopping with you, but it'll be your show, babe." He pulled up into the parking lot at the mall closest to his place, down at the end with the Subway.

"But why? I don't understand."

"Because we can't live on pizza and take-out, babe. And because you need routine."

"I like pizza." Justin got out of the car, inhaled. "Smells good."

"You can't eat just pizza, though. Besides, I bet we can learn to make it." He led the way to the Subway.

Justin got a sandwich heavy on the veggies and turkey, foregoing the chips.

He ordered the same for himself and they settled at a little table by the windows. "You're eating healthy now that you're not having pizza."

"You know I like sandwiches with crunch."

He did. He also knew that Justin loved oatmeal and eggs, and that the man adored pasta. "I do. I know more about you than any other person on earth."

"You do." Justin didn't look worried.

He smiled across at his boy. What would Justin say if Chris told him he knew more about Justin than Justin did?

"How's your sandwich?" Justin asked.

"It makes an awesome change from pizza."

Justin stuck his tongue out.

"Don't stick that out if you aren't going to use it."

"I already used it."

Chris threw his head back and laughed.

Justin snorted, finished his sandwich. "Man, I should have gotten the foot long."

"That's the swimming." He handed a twenty over. "Go get yourself another one."

"You sure? You want anything?"

"I think I saw cookies up there."

"I'll grab you one." Justin headed back to the counter, laughing and talking to the guy behind the bar.

Already his boy was happier than when Justin had first called. Hell, he was happier today than he'd been yesterday. Give him a few weeks and the weight would be off Justin's back.

Justin needed the pool, his routine, and him. Luckily, he could give his babe all three.

Chapter Eleven

Justin woke up and stretched, back popping, naked body sliding on the sheets. He'd been dreaming about swimming, about cutting through the water. A warm hand slid along his side and curled around his hip.

"Mmm. Morning." He let Chris encourage him down for another snuggle.

Coach pulled them together, nuzzling into his neck. Chris' hair was soft, thick, warm on his fingers. He felt the heat of Chris' breath and then of Chris' tongue, licking at his collarbones. He chuckled, the warmth and gentle tickle perfect. Chris' smile felt good against his skin.

"I like waking up with you," he noted idly.

"It's good isn't it?" Chris' hand slid across his belly.

"It is. So good."

Chris leaned into him, took his lips. Justin moaned, the kiss slow and lazy, easy and endless. It turned the morning into a wonderful thing. He slowly stroked Chris' chest, belly, fingers trailing.

"Mmm. I like the direction this is going."

"I like lazy mornings." His fingertips brushed the tip of Chris' cock.

"Uh-huh." Chris pushed toward his hand, into his touch.

Justin snuggled in, eyes closing as he slowly jacked Chris off, fingers moving up and down along the shaft.

Chris reached up to finger his right nipple. God, he was aching there, so tender. Back and forth went that finger, then Chris started using his fingernail. He rumbled, shook his head. So much.

Chris took his mouth, tongue pushing in as Chris began to tug lightly on the same nipple. His touch around Chris' cock hiccupped, then he squeezed harder, hand moving faster. Fingers sliding, Chris moved to his other nipple, rubbing his thumb into it. The touches weren't too much, weren't enough to shock him or bring him out of this soft, quiet space.

The kiss ended and Chris kissed his way down to Justin's left nipple. He tensed, and sure enough, Chris' mouth wrapped around his flesh, suction making him ache, just a little. Chris eased him back on the mattress, hands moving over his skin, trailing over his belly and pushing hard enough that he had to relax.

The suction around his left nipple got harder, his flesh swelling up for Chris. Oh, fuck. That ached, so good. It went on and on, the ache building slowly.

"Chris..." He was hard, and his balls felt heavy.

Humming, Chris finally let his nipple go, only to move to the other one and wrap hot lips around it. Somehow he was still holding onto Chris' cock, Chris' hips pushing the heat along his palm. He hadn't even noticed, he was so caught in pleasure. The thrusts came in time with Chris' suction, the thick cock almost throbbing in time with his nipple. He arched, pushed up toward Chris' body, wanting friction on his prick.

Chris pulled off his nipple, checking both closely before nodding, grinning. "Perfect."

"P...perfect?" His thumb rubbing the tip of Chris' cock, sliding the slick pre-come around.

Chris groaned, jerked for him. "Nice and swollen. Red. Mine." Chris kissed his right nipple. "Wanna suck each other off?"

"Yes." He turned, groaning as he rubbed against Chris, the sheets.

Chris grabbed his hips and held on tight, fingers digging into his skin. Licking softly, Chris bathed his prick. His thighs spread, and he grabbed Chris' hips, dragging his lover in. Chris' moan vibrated against his prick, and then the head of his prick was wrapped in heat.

"Coach..." He responded in kind, licking a line around the tip of that fine cock.

Chris' tongue slapped at his slit. He grunted, sucked Chris in, pulling hard. Chris' hips bucked, pushing his prick deeper. He buried his nose in the soft, heaviness of Chris' balls, inhaling the warm, familiar scent. One soft moan after another vibrated his prick as Chris sucked him. They rocked together, and it was almost sweet, totally easy, to love on each other like that.

Chris' hands landed on his ass, fingers sliding on his crack. He hummed, swallowing around the tip of Chris' cock. Chris' gasp nearly lost his cock. Oh, yeah. He swallowed again, and again, pulling hard. Chris began sucking just as hard, matching his rhythm. He nodded, soaring, aching to come.

Chris pushed a finger into his ass. Uhn. Justin's legs spread, wide. Chris sucked, finger pushing deep into him. He rode the touch, sucking hard, pulling with all his might. Chris pushed another finger in and hit his gland. Justin cried out, fingers digging into Chris' thighs. Chris hit his gland again, and then again.

"Coach!" Chris' cock popped out of his mouth, and he shot.

Chris drank him down, still sucking to beat the band. Oh. Oh, fuck. Oh, fuck. He sobbed, fucking Chris' lips. Chris encouraged it, fingers moving in and out, filling him over and over.

"Please. Please." He was still hard, still aching.

Golden

"Roll over, babe."

He moved, eager, needy for whatever Chris would give him. Chris' fingers slid back into him, slick now, stretching. Justin nodded, spread, letting Chris in. Those fingers weren't in him for long before they slid away and then it was Chris' cock, spreading him even wider. The pressure was deep, filling him, pushing him and he spread.

"Fucking love you, Justin."

"Chris." Oh, he wanted to believe that.

"Love. You." Chris thrust in with each word, hitting his gland.

"Yes. Don't stop. Please."

"Not stopping." No, Chris moved even faster, taking him harder.

He took Chris in and in, moaning, his cock achingly hard again. One hand dropped from his hips to wrap around his prick, closing the circle of pleasure. All he could do was nod, moan, share his pleasure. Chris kept pumping into him, the thick cock so good.

"Sweet. So fucking good."

"Uh-huh." Chris pushed in harder.

His body tensed, so close, so tight. Chris' fingers pushed against his slit on the next thrust. He came again, shaking with it, flying. Chris cried out, filling him with heat.

"Oh, God. Oh, God..." Justin panted, just overwhelmed.

Chris pulled out and pulled him down, Coach wrapping around him and holding on. He caught his breath, melted, happy.

"Morning, babe."

"Morning, Coach."

"Mmm... let me know when you're ready to talk about today's punishments."

"Hmm?" What? No way.

148

"You heard me. And you knew this was coming. It was why we made the rules in the first place."

"This sucks. I didn't do anything wrong."

"Except break the rules that we clearly set out the other day."

"What? When? What did I do?"

"The big thing was the running yourself down you were doing yesterday."

"When?" Had he? Yesterday? Bullshit.

"In the laundry room at the pool."

"I was yelling at you."

"You were putting yourself down while you were yelling at me."

Well... well, what the fuck was he supposed to say to that?

"I think three swats are fair," Chris suggested.

"I don't like this idea." Three swats, though, he could handle that.

"We've talked about this. We made a list and I was clear we'd started."

"I still don't like it."

"Well, of course not. It's a punishment."

His lips opened, closed, opened again. Chris chuckled and kissed him, tongue slipping into his mouth. Before he knew it, Chris had him over his lap, hand on his ass. The first swat was shocking, the second less so and the third almost painful. As soon as Chris stopped, he was up and moving, off the bed, toward the shower.

"No." Chris' voice cracked out, stopping him in is tracks.

"What?"

"Come back here."

He wrapped his arms around his belly. "Why?"

"Because you're missing the best part about punishments."

"The best part?" He wanted a hug, so fucking bad.

"Come here, J." Chris held out a hand. He went, like he was drawn over. Chris pulled him back onto the bed, holding him close. "The best part of a punishment is after, when I hold you."

Justin didn't know what to say, so he didn't. He sat there, cuddling in. Chris slid his hand down and rubbed Justin's ass, making it tingle.

"How does it feel?"

"Embarrassing."

"No, Justin. This is nothing to be embarrassed about. Does it tingle at all when I rub it? Ache?"

He nodded, hiding his face in Chris' shoulder.

"A good ache, isn't it?" Chris squeezed his ass, fingers digging in.

"Uh...uh-huh." It shouldn't be good, but it was.

"And there's nothing wrong with that." Chris swatted again. "Sometimes we'll do it just for fun." Chris' lips were on his throat. "Sometimes we'll do it because we need it; we need the heat and the way it makes us feel." His ass was squeezed again. "Sometimes you'll ask for it and sometimes you'll act up so the punishment comes."

No. No way. No way at all.

Chris gave him a knowing look. "You will. You'll see."

"I don't know what to do, man."

"Just accept it. You'll learn about it as we go."

That actually seemed liked the easiest answer on earth, so he nodded.

"My brave, beautiful, talented boy."

The soft praise made him blush, but if felt amazing.

"Now we've made sure your sweet nips are nice and swollen. We've dealt with the punishments. What comes next?"

"The rewards?" That sounded better.

"Yes. That's our routine. Make sure your nips are good

and swollen, punishments, rewards from the day before."

"Okay..." Okay, rewards.

"Yes. I think you deserve one. You did well yesterday."

"Thank you, Coach."

"What do you think would be an appropriate reward?"

"I... What are rewards?" This whole thing was so new.

"Well, really, that's up to us. For some people, it would be more spanking." Chris' eyes were twinkling.

"But that was the punishment..."

Chris' hand landed on his butt again, just tapping, warm. "But for some people it's also the reward." Chris tapped his ass again.

"Not sane people." His breath came a little faster.

"No? You don't think so?" Two more gentle swats followed, really beginning to warm him.

He moaned, his entire body supported by Chris.

"I think it's feeling pretty good to you right now." Chris' voice was low, soft, that hand still working him. His lips were on Chris' throat, the gentle heat and ache so sexual, sensual. "You think I should stop, babe?"

"You'll let it just feel good?"

"It's a reward, babe, of course it's going to be good."

"Okay." He let his eyes close.

It did feel good, too, the constant, slow... he didn't even think you could call it spanking. He went with it, though, rocking, moaning deep in his chest. His ass got hotter and hotter, the burn building slowly.

"Love you, J. So much."

"Coach..." Oh, fuck. Fuck, more.

"Mmm." Chris didn't stop, just kept swatting him lightly, over and over.

His poor prick began to fill again. Crazy. Crazy. No one could come so much.

"Mmm. A good reward, isn't it?"

Justin squeezed his eyes closed, but nodded. Yes. Fuck.

Groaning, Chris kept it up, the heat incredible now.

"Please. Please, I don't know what to do, Coach."

"How does it feel, babe?"

"Hot."

"And you like it."

He didn't answer. He couldn't.

"You should come. You should rub off against me and come."

"Again?" He already had, twice.

"Yep."

"Coach... I'm gonna hurt my balls." He felt like a teenager, coming over and over.

"Don't worry about your balls."

The taps were still happening and he found himself gasping for air, the room spinning. Chris' breath warmed his face, the soft lips pressing over his skin.

"Please. Please. Help me."

"Come on, babe, come for me one more time."

"One more..." Justin sobbed softly, their lips meeting.

Chris' tongue pushed into his mouth, one finger rubbing against his hole. Heat spread between them, and he sobbed, totally exhausted, worn.

"I've got you, babe. I've so got you."

He was eased back onto the mattress, held, covered. "Mmm. See? Spanking isn't necessarily a bad thing."

Justin didn't answer; he just cuddled in, trying to remember how to breathe.

"You're amazing, Justin. Simply amazing." The covers were pulled back up, Chris wrapped around him like a heated blanket.

They rested together, dark and safe. Close.

Chapter Twelve

Come on, Just. Put on your glad rags, we're going out."

It had been a great week, Justin working with him, swimming. A grand first week together and Chris felt like celebrating.

"Out? Okay. Like jeans and t-shirt out or khakis and button down out?"

"Khakis and button down out. We're going to the Lumiere." He was pulling out all the stops.

"Oh, man. For real? Steaks and lobster?"

"Yep. We're celebrating."

"Celebrating what?" Justin stripped off his shirt, opened his jeans, exposing that flat, ripped belly.

"Your first week at work, our first week as a couple."

"Oh, okay. That's cool." Justin wriggled out of his jeans, popped them in the dirty clothes pile.

"Mmm." Damn, but Justin had a sweet body.

Justin grabbed the deodorant, checked his stubble in the mirror.

"I like it." He stepped up behind Justin and stroked one rough cheek.

"I do too." He leaned in, rubbed Chris' palm.

"Mmm." He rubbed up against Justin's ass, his prick beginning to firm up.

"That's my butt."

Yes, yes, he knew. He appreciated it, too, sort of bone deep. "Uh-huh." He slid his hands down to Justin's hips, pulled Justin back against him. He'd never had the opportunity to look at his boy like that—covered with a dusting of near-black hair, fuzzy and cut. "Gorgeous boy."

"You're biased."

"So?" Wasn't everyone?

Justin snorted. "I guess you have a point."

"I do." He rubbed his prick against Justin's ass. One of them was overdressed.

"This isn't helping me get dressed, you know." Justin was laughing at him.

"And here I was thinking I should be getting undressed."

"Do they let us eat naked?"

He laughed, bit Justin's neck. "Somehow I don't think so."

"No. No, I don't either." Justin shivered and he could see the man's cock leap and jerk.

"It's a bit of a turn on, though, isn't it? Imagining doing it in public, maybe getting caught."

"I don't know about that." Maybe not, but the fantasy was there, lifting that sweet prick.

"Not every fantasy has to work in reality for it to be a turn on." Chris wrapped one hand around Justin's cock, just lightly, hefting it.

"No?" Justin leaned back against him, smiled. "God, I love your hands."

"They love you, too, babe." He let his free one wander down to cup Justin's balls as he tightened his hold on the long prick. He tugged a little, offering a little hint of ache, and Justin spread for him. So eager for every sensation, for that hint of kink and more. "Imagine me jacking you under the cover of the table."

"Coach..." Justin turned, lips on his jaw.

"Yeah, J?" He lifted his head, letting Justin have his throat.

"You smell good." Justin moaned for him, stubble rasping him.

"Thank you. You smell like mine."

Justin moaned, still licking and nuzzling him. Chris kept stroking the pretty cock, rubbing his slacks covered one against Justin's ass. So many games he needed to play with Justin, so many wonderful things to explore. For now, it would be a quickie before they went out.

"Do you think anyone would notice if I did it? If I got you off right there in the middle of the restaurant?" He increased the movement of his hand.

"I'd be quiet. I'm good at that."

Oh, fuck, yes. "Yes, you can be, can't you?" He kept stroking, rubbing the tip of Justin's prick. His pretty boy nodded, thighs tightening, deep red nipples drawn up. "We should do it. Tonight. I'll make you come and no one will know."

His boy shook his head, moaned.

"We could. In between the appetizer and entrees."

"You're perverse."

"And you love it." He pushed his thumb into Justin's slit. Justin jerked, went up on tiptoe, rocked. He tugged Justin back in close. "Gonna make you shoot."

"Uhn." Justin's head fell forward, throat working hard.

"Yeah, we're almost there now." He worked the slit, stroking Justin, making it burn. "Can you picture it? Feeling like you do right now in a room full of strangers who haven't a clue? That waiter could come by again, at any moment, and catch us."

"Chris..." Justin shivered, swallowing hard.

"You're allowed to come, boy." He squeezed a little

tighter and jacked faster. He bit Justin's earlobe, tugging hard. "Come on, babe. Show me how hot I make you."

"Oh, God." Justin humped up, spunk spraying over his fingers.

That smell was fantastic, going through him and making him need. His boy leaned back, throat working, body sheened with sweat.

"Mmm." Chris rubbed Justin's come into his skin.

He loved how debauched Justin looked like this, how open and sated. There was a mark coming up on Justin's chest where he'd bitten, and Chris smiled to see it. He traced the mark, loving how the simple touch made Justin's cock jerk.

"Mmm. Just look at you. You take my breath."

"You... you want me? I can feel that you're hard."

"I am and I always want you. The question is, do I want to savor the want or sate it."

Justin nodded. "Sometimes the ache is good, huh?"

"It is indeed." He loved the Justin was getting it, now. Learning to need. "I'm going to wait. You need to get dressed so we can make our reservations."

"Okay. Okay, let me clean up. Two minutes."

"No more than that. I don't want to be parted from you."

Justin gave him a heated, wide-eyed look.

"Hurry, boy."

"Okay. Okay, sorry." Justin ran some water, washing himself off.

He chuckled, watching happily as Justin used a washcloth and started to get dressed. A pair of slacks, a nice shirt were pulled out.

"Mmm. You clean up well."

"Thanks." Justin dressed quickly, even splashed on a little cologne.

When his boy was done, Chris got up and went over

to him, giving Justin his arm. "Shall we?"

"Absolutely." Justin took his offer, and leaned in to kiss him. "Thank you for the invitation."

"It's my pleasure, babe."

Smiling, even more on the inside than the outside, he took his boy out.

Chapter Thirteen

The fucking world was making him grumpy, and he left a note for Chris that he was going to swim it off, then he'd run the silly errands they needed done and come home in a less bitchtastic mood. He jogged to the pool, sweating hard by the time he got there, showered, and dove into the water.

By the time he was on his third set of laps, the tension and stress was gone, worked out and leaving him focused on nothing but the next turn. About then, someone cut through the water next to him, strokes strong. It didn't take half a dozen strokes before he recognized Chris, and he smiled. Why wasn't he surprised?

Chris matched him for awhile, and then slowly fell back. He didn't worry about it; this was him time, his place. His world. It felt good, though, knowing the man he passed in the lanes was Chris.

By the time the whistle sounded, he was getting tired and hungry, needing a big bottle of water, and he stopped without complaint.

Coach handed over a towel and his water, giving him a grin. "You feeling better, J?"

"Yeah. Yeah, I am." He sucked the water down, loose and easy in his skin.

"You're looking good out there."

"Thanks. Feels good."

"Real good, I bet." Coach smiled at him.

"Yep." He toweled off. "How're you?"

"Glad to have my boy back."

"Back?" He caught his breath, loving the well-exercised feeling.

"You were a bit of a growly monster this morning after your punishments and rewards."

"Yeah. I woke up in a bad mood, I guess. I felt... like my skin didn't fit." The whole punishment and reward thing was... still very uncomfortable. Very.

"Swimming put you right, though, eh?'

"It did."

"Good deal."

It was. Justin nodded, leaned back on his elbows.

"You ready for your first cooking lesson today?"

"Nope." Not really.

Chris grinned. "What have you got against cooking?"

He shrugged. "I don't know, nothing, I guess. I mean, I've never done it."

"So there's every possibility you're going to love it."

"I doubt it, but there's a chance." He loved swimming.

"Well if that's going to be your attitude..."

"Well, what? We've paid for the classes. We have to go."

"Well, if that's your attitude, then you aren't going to like it. You need to keep an open mind."

"I'm trying." He rolled his eyes. "Besides, we'll be together. That's fun."

"Oh, yes, the enthusiasm is practically rolling off you." Chris flicked a towel at him.

"Hey!" He shrugged. "I don't know, man. It's a little outside anything I know, and food... it's like such a big deal for everyone."

"That's because we all have to have it to eat. It's kind of like breathing."

"Well, I know that." He stood up, frustrated. "I hope we get to make pizza."

Chris laughed. "Oh, I do love you, Justin."

"I know." He stretched. "Are you... I know we had errands. Did you want to do them together or do you have other plans?"

"I'm at your disposal."

"I like that." Their eyes met and they both smiled and it felt so good. "Let's run through the showers and head out."

Cooking lessons. The things he did for love. Justin shook his head at himself. Love. Yeah.

"Works for me." Coach reached out, fingers brushing his left nipple.

"Hey." They couldn't do that, not here in the pool. "Be good."

"We're the only ones here, boy."

"Still, it's not cool."

"I'm easy." Coach headed toward the change room, towel handing off one shoulder.

"I've heard that about you." He couldn't help the tease.

Chris put his head back and laughed. He stopped, watched. Yeah. Stupid in love. That was him.

Turning around, Chris tilted his head. "You coming, Just?"

"Uh-huh." He couldn't be positive, but he thought Chris' smile was rather knowing.

"Grinning at me. We have shit to do. Go get cleaned up."

Chris nodded. "You go get cleaned up. You were swimming longer than me. Probably have chlorine in your veins."

"If I'm lucky." Justin grinned. That would be him, if he was a superhero. Chlorine Man.

That had Chris laughing again, the man stripping out of his swimming trunks and heading for the showers.

Cooking classes. Him. Wow. Good thing he loved the weird son of a bitch.

The cooking class had been fun. Justin hadn't admitted it yet, but Chris could tell. Then they'd gone shopping, teasing as they'd picked up the ingredients for the spaghetti Bolognese that they'd learned that afternoon.

Justin was making it for supper. Chris was in the kitchen for moral support alone. And because Justin looked fucking sexy in an apron.

His boy wasn't stupid and loved a challenge. And eating. He had a hunch once Justin had a few meals under his belt, he wasn't going to want to have pizza unless it was homemade. He hoped so anyway. Justin preparing supper was in the rules now.

Chris knew Justin wasn't getting it, not yet, but it would come. It had to.

"You want me to set the table for you tonight?"

"I guess so, sure. That would be cool." Justin looked nervous, staring at all the ingredients. "You sure you want this? You just tasted it earlier. I could order something."

He chuckled. "The point is you're learning to cook so we don't have to order. Make the spaghetti." He figured if worse came to worst, they could just eat the spaghetti with butter.

Justin flipped him off, but it was playful, teasing, and he was hustled out of the kitchen.

"You don't want moral support? How about immoral support?"

"Out. You'll tease me."

"Would I do that?" He went, though, because yeah, he would.

"You're an ass. You so would."

"I have an ass," Chris called back, laughing as he settled in the living room. Man, it was hard not watching, not being there. Boring, too.

Part of this was spending time with Justin. Talking. Watching. He'd give Justin five minutes to get his bearings and then he'd join his lover. This sitting on the living room alone just wasn't any fun.

He must have glanced at his watch twenty times before five minutes had passed. Finally, though, he was able to get up and head back into the kitchen. It actually smelled pretty good, Justin methodically going through notes, repeating the steps from class. Of course they might not eat until tomorrow...

Chris didn't tease, though. The time would come when he would. Probably soon.

"I thought you were going to sit in the living room." Justin was crumbling up the meat.

"I got bored. No teasing, I promise."

"Okay. I'm following the recipe." And quite carefully, too.

"It smells good," he offered, because it did.

"You think so?"

"Don't you?"

Justin almost smiled. "Yeah."

He nodded. "Yeah. It smells like spaghetti."

"Well, given that's what I'm supposed to be cooking, that's cool."

He chuckled. "You look good, like you know what you're doing."

"Thank you." He got a smile, warm, almost happy. "Do you want to make a salad?"

"Was that on the recipe cards?" Okay, so he couldn't wait until later to tease.

"No, but we like salad."

He chuckled, going to the fridge. They'd bought one of those packages that had all the stuff in it for making Caesar salad.

The lid went on the sauce; the pasta water was checked. It was fucking sexy, watching Justin cook. The man wasn't confident, but he managed, he was paying attention, trying. Chris didn't think it would be long before Justin was good at this.

He grabbed the salad bag and then a bowl from the cupboard.

"Do you want wine?"

"Did we get any?" He didn't remember grabbing any while they'd made the grocery run. Besides, Justin wasn't supposed to be drinking unless he said it was okay and he thought it was too early to relax that rule. Justin needed to drink to enjoy it, not to dull worries or life or anything.

"Uh..." Justin tilted his head. "We'd talked about getting some for the sauce, but... Did you get any?"

"Nope. No drinking, remember? Your recipe said red wine or red wine vinegar." And he didn't need to drink, let alone do it in front of Justin. His boy had the beginning of a real problem and he was going to control it. "Water? We've got sparkling and tap."

"I want tea, I think."

"Okay. I'll have water. Tap." He gave Justin a wink and started opening bags, putting the salad together. "There's a lot of fucking plastic here. How hard could it be to figure this out without getting it premade?"

"It's lettuce, right? Lettuce lives with the bagged salad."

"Uh-huh." He put the salad together, poured on the sauce and tossed it. They'd make their own next time. He'd bet it would be cheaper anyway, to buy a pot of salad dressing and a head or two of lettuce instead of the pre-made stuff.

Justin put the pasta in the water and started the timer. Chris put the salad on the table and then set it with two place settings and wandered for the next seven minutes as Justin worried over the pasta. It was finally deemed ready, and Justin put the sauce on the table and drained the pasta, set it out as well.

"Looks nice." Justin grabbed the bread and put it in the oven.

"It does. I'm proud of you—our first homemade meal."

"Yeah? Maybe you should wait 'til you taste it." Still, Justin looked pleased with himself.

Chris shook his head. "If it tasted like shit, it would smell like shit."

"You think so?" Justin opened the oven and rolled his eyes, set the incredibly well-toasted bread on the table.

"I think so." He grinned and pulled Justin's chair out for him.

"Thank you." Justin blushed, but the smile was worth it.

Chris let his fingers linger on Justin's shoulders after his babe was sitting. "It really does look good, Justin."

"I hope it's good. It was sort of fun."

"I'm glad." It would suck if Justin hated it. Of course, he'd had a pretty good hunch that wouldn't be the case.

He sat and they filled the plates. It wasn't amazing, but it absolutely wasn't bad at all. It sure beat pizza or Chinese or burgers for the five hundredth time. "I can't believe this is your first time cooking, J. it's great."

Look at his boy beam. This had been a good idea, even if he did say so himself. Being able to cook was going to help Justin with his self-esteem, let him realize he was good at more than just swimming.

They ate, chatted, and Justin actually relaxed for him, and when it was time to clean the kitchen, they worked together. He grabbed a couple bottles of water and they wandered into the living room together.

"You want to watch TV?" Justin asked.

"I want to reward you for a job well-done."

"Okay..." He got a curious look. "What does that mean?"

"It means I want to make love to you, J. Maybe put a kinky twist on it."

"Oh. You're a horndog." He got the grin he wanted, though.

"I'm a horndog in love, babe. With you." He tugged Justin in close, rubbed their hips and their noses together.

Justin's eyes cut away, the man's cheeks rosy, then he got a kiss, a short, hard kiss.

"I'm going to keep saying it," he promised.

He got another kiss. "Hush."

"No, not hush. I love you."

"You can't."

Chris stopped short in the act of leaning in for another kiss. "I do."

"I do too."

"What?" Now he was confused.

Justin pulled away, looked at him. "I love you, too."

Oh..." He hadn't been expecting it, not at all. But it warmed him, all the way through. He felt the smile spreading over his face.

"You want a cup of coffee?" Justin asked.

"No, I want a cup of Justin."

"I won't fit in a cup."

"Then I'll just have to have all of you."

Justin touched his wrist. "Is it going to be weird, being in love?"

"Why would it be weird?"

"I've never been with someone I was in love with."

"You've been with me for a few weeks now."

165

"I have, but I didn't know I was in love with you for sure."

"Well now things can only be better because you do know." He tugged Justin in, kissed his babe. Justin tasted like their dinner.

Justin wrapped one hand around the back of his neck, tugged him in, tongue sliding against him. Humming, he deepened the kiss, his hands sliding over Justin's hips and around to his ass. Justin took a half step forward, moaned into his lips. He tugged Justin in closer, rubbing them together. Hungry boy. Needy man.

"Too many clothes," he noted, wondering if Justin would take the initiative to do something about that.

"Mmmhmm." Justin tugged his shirt out of his slacks.

Moaning at the touch of Justin's fingers on his skin, he returned the favor, working slowly to remove Justin's t-shirt from his jeans. His swimmer was so fine, ab muscles rolling as Justin sucked in. He stopped to stroke them, to tease the smooth skin, the tiny treasure trail that disappeared into Justin's jeans. It was so hot, the way those muscles jerked and jumped under his touch. He dragged the fingernails of his right hand down over them.

"Hey..." Justin gasped, kissed him even as one hand wrapped around his wrist.

"Is for horses," he managed, twisting his hand in Justin's grip and winding their fingers together.

Justin moaned, tongue sliding over his lips.

"You like the slight sting of pain, Justin." He used his free hand to scrape over Justin's belly again. Justin liked aching.

He pressed over the sweet, barely there welts his fingernails had left. The tanned skin goose pimpled up, muscles jerking and jumping. Fuck, it made him hard how wonderfully Justin's body responded to him. He wanted to push, wanted to make Justin twist. He slid his fingers up toward Justin's swollen, beautifully abused nipples.

"Don't..."

"I have to." He flicked both nipples at the same time.

"Wh...why?" Justin arched, cock filling in the tight jeans.

"Because I love the way you move when I touch them." Because he loved how sensitive they were. Because he loved how Justin had to notice them. "Sexy boy." He pinched one nipple.

Justin grunted, jerked away from him.

"Where are you going?" He tugged Justin back in, sliding the t-shirt up and off so he could lean in and suck on those pretty nipples.

"Away from your fingers."

He laughed softly. "You love it."

"I love you."

"So you said. I like hearing it."

"Yeah?" Justin looked so... pleased.

"Yeah. I like hearing it a whole lot. Makes me feel good."

"Makes me feel pretty good, too."

"Excellent." Chris leaned in to flick his tongue across the tip of Justin's right nipple.

Justin's soft moan was pure sex. He took the little nipple between his lips and tugged. Justin's hands wrapped around his head, held on. Humming, he tugged harder, licked and sucked.

"Don't. Aches. Damn it."

He let go of the nipple and rubbed it with his nose. Justin's gasp made him grin. Kissing his way over, he moved to Justin's left nipple.

"You're obsessed."

"Uh-huh. Someone should be."

Justin shook his head, fingers tangling in his hair.

"Yes. They deserve love and attention." He began

sucking on the left nipple, gently to start with. He loved the way it hardened beneath his tongue.

"Can't we sit down?"

"Knees giving out?" He smiled against Justin's skin.

"Your neck's going to hurt."

Oh, little shit.

"I think I can survive it."

Justin chuckled, stepped away. "You're a dork. Come on, let's sit."

"I'm not a dork," he complained, following Justin to the couch.

"Yep. A dork."

"I don't think that's allowed, you know. Calling your coach and your Top a dork."

"You're not my coach anymore."

"Not at the moment, but I am your Top." It was similar. Besides, Justin would be competing again. He was sure of it now.

"Maybe." He got a teasing wink.

He growled a little, bit Justin's left nipple.

"Ow!" Justin pulled away, keeping distance between them.

He grabbed Justin's hips and tugged him closer. "Are you hard, babe?"

"You make me harder than anyone else ever."

"That's because I know what you want." And he was leaning, more and more, what Justin needed. "So let me grab your nipples, eh?" He demonstrated by tugging on the right one this time.

He didn't squeeze hard; he let the pressure be slow, steady, and Justin moaned, moving almost into this lap. He slid his free hand around one of Justin's hips, encouraging Justin to move, to rock against him. That got Justin in his lap, pushed close, belly hot against him.

"You make me need, babe. So hard."

"You're amazing. No one ever wanted so much."

"Clearly you've been having sex with inferior guys," he teased, though it was the truth if the guys Justin had been with hadn't seen his sexy boy for what he was.

"I haven't been having a lot of sex."

"Before me."

Justin rolled his eyes. "Well, yeah."

Chris leaned in and bit Justin's right nipple for rolling his eyes at him.

"Ow!" Justin pulled his hair. "You're so mean."

"You love it." He wrapped his hand around Justin's prick, tugging the lovely hard on.

"Do not." Justin arched back for him, lips parted, hungry. God, look at his boy.

"No, you're right. You don't love it at all." He kept stroking, thumb sliding across the sweet tip on every up stroke.

"God, your hands. I used to imagine..."

"Tell me." He wanted to know Justin's fantasies.

Justin shook his head. "Just stuff. I just wanted you."

"There's no just about that, Just." He frowned. "Wait...." He chuckled. "I know what I meant."

Justin's laugh rang out, warm and happy. God, he loved that sound. He blew on Justin's right nipple.

"Mmm." Justin hummed, fingers sliding through his hair.

He wrapped a hand around Justin's prick, thumb pushing against the slit as he played with the round head. He kept the touch light, he wanted this to drag out, he wanted Justin sensitive and aching. Then he slid his hand down to roll Justin's balls.

"Mmm." Justin kissed his ear, lips wrapping around the lobe to suck.

Groaning, he slid his fingers in behind those sweet balls, stroking the hot skin.

"Feels good." Justin tugged his earlobe with careful teeth.

He jerked and pressed closer, mouth wrapping around Justin's left nipple and sucking strongly. Justin's head fell back, hips rolling, cock hard as iron as it leaked against him. His babe might protest, but he loved the burn and ache in his nipples. He slid a hand back between Justin's thighs, stroking the sensitive skin between them, and then the sweet, heavy sacs. A ring would be perfect there, private, hidden. His.

"Gonna pierce you, Just. Give you a ring nobody can see, nobody but us will know is there."

"You are?"

"I am." He let his fingers wander back to that sweet patch behind Justin's balls. "Right here."

"If you do it. Only you."

Chris thought about that. He had the internet, he could buy a needle and the ring, and he had steady hands. He nodded.

"Okay." Justin rested their foreheads together. "I trust you."

Heat moved through him at the words. "Thank you, babe."

Justin kissed him again, this time almost chaste. He let Justin lead the gentle kiss for awhile, and then took over, devouring his babe's mouth. His beautiful lover. His swimmer. His boy.

"This is going to be a part of our routine, babe. You'll make supper, we'll clean it up, and then make love."

"What if we don't want to make love?"

He hoped his expression told Justin he thought the man was crazy.

"What?" Justin was fighting laughter, he could tell. "It could happen!"

"It's possible, just not probable."

"Maybe I'll turn straight." Justin was just barely holding back the laughter and Chris loved it, loved the joy he could see.

He managed to bite back his own laughter. "How can you turn straight? Turning implies a bend, right?"

"I would go with flip. I could... flip straight." Justin lost it, hooting with laughter.

"Flip straight." Chris snorted and started laughing, too.

"Uh-huh." Justin leaned into him, chest bouncing with his chuckles.

"You couldn't flip straight anymore than I could beat you in a race in the water."

Justin snorted. "That's not going to happen."

"Exactly."

Justin kissed the end of his nose. "It's good to laugh, huh?"

"It is, babe. Very good."

Justin settled against him, leaning. "I've missed you."

"I'm right here, babe."

"I know." Justin shrugged. "I'm glad."

"Me, too." He kissed the top of Justin's head, enjoying the moment.

Chris found himself holding on, just letting Justin rest against him. It didn't suck. It didn't suck at all.

Chapter Fourteen

Justin looked at the recipe in the book. It didn't make sense. It didn't. He rubbed his forehead and looked at the words again, watching them swim on the white paper. Oh, fuck, his head hurt.

"Coach." He headed out of the kitchen. "Coach, I need you."

"In here, Just." Coach's voice came from the living room.

He stumbled in, swaying. "Coach." Migraine. Migraine. The flashing lights started up and he winced, trying to hide from them. Chris would help him. Chris knew what to do.

"Shit, Justin. Migraine?" Coach came over and put a hand over his eyes, the warmth and darkness helping a tiny bit. "Okay, Let's get you into the bathroom, you need a warm, dark shower." Chris spoke gently, quietly.

Justin groaned, leaned into the touch. "Help me."

"I've got you, babe." Chris led him into the bathroom and didn't turn on the lights, just set him to sit on the edge of the tub and got the hot water on, then helped him in.

He groaned again, tears sliding down his cheeks. God. God, he felt like shit.

Chris held him, the hot water pounding down on him. "Breathe, babe."

"Hurts." He held on, knowing that Coach had been

with him through these before.

"Shh. No talking, just breathing." Those strong hands began to work his shoulders, his neck, and the back of his head.

He started to relax, then the nausea hit him and he pushed up, making the commode as he lost it. Chris kept holding him, eased him back into the water when he was done. Better.

Coach didn't try to talk to him, or make him do anything, just held him, soothed him in the warm wet dark. Justin dozed off, Coach's arms around him even as they sank to the bottom of the tub.

He woke up when Coach started moving him again. "Hot's running out."

"Uh-huh." He stood up, swaying a little, his head feeling too light.

"Let's get you to bed."

"Stay with me?"

"I will, babe."

"Thank you." They curled together in bed, Justin hiding his face in Chris' chest. It was quiet and dark and warm and Chris' hands moved so gently over him. "Sorry." It felt so much better.

"Shh." Chris continued to touch him with those warm, sure hands.

He dozed, floated, periodically coming up from his crazy dreams before sinking again. Chris was there every time he came up, too, keeping it dark and warm and safe.

"Love." A straw pushed in his lips, cold water so bright it was almost shocking.

"Just a bit," murmured Chris, the words careful and soft.

"Thank you." He thought about opening his eyes, then thought different.

"Just relax, Justin. You don't need to do anything but

rest and get better."

"I'm sorry. I was going to cook, but..." The migraine had hit so fast.

"You're exempt if you're sick, babe."

He hummed, nuzzling in. "I tried."

"I know. I saw."

"Thank you for your help."

"Shh. Just rest. I know it flares back up if you get moving too soon."

"Yeah." Migraines sucked. He wasn't sure why he got them, and they didn't happen often, but when they did, ick. And also ow.

"I've got some wonton soup we can warm up when you're feeling up to testing out your stomach."

"Okay. Okay, maybe. Maybe you'd cook me eggs?"

"Yeah? I could probably manage some eggs."

"I like your eggs." They were like... home.

"This is just revenge for making you cook suppers." He could tell Chris was pleased, though, the words teasing, the look in Coach's eyes warm.

"Yep. My brain exploded." He winked, reached out and twined their fingers together.

Chris chuckled for him, tugging him closer and nuzzling the top of his head. "It's better now, though, yeah?"

"Yeah. Just feels weird and tingly, you know how that is."

"Luckily I only know because you've told me and not from experience. I'd take it from you if I could, though." Chris' hands were so warm where they touched him.

"Mmm." He just let himself enjoy it, float, nice and easy.

Soft sounds slid over his skin as Chris pressed kisses against his shoulder, his throat. There was no pressure from Chris to do anything, none at all, despite the heat he could feel against his thigh. He let himself just melt, enjoy the care, the love that he could feel in every touch. Chris' touches slowed, the big hands just resting against his skin now, warm breath pushing against his neck.

"I love you." Justin let the words float there.

He felt Chris' smile against his skin.

Chris had him, and it was okay.

Good, even.

Real.

Chapter Fifteen

Chris waited for Justin to do up his belt and started the car, aiming for home. Justin's hair was still wet from his swim, his cheeks bright from effort. His babe looked happy and that made his heart glad.

"We need to stop at the grocery store for dinner supplies?"

"I don't think so. I was thinking we could just grill some hot dogs and sit outside on the porch."

"That actually sounds nice. We have hot dogs?"

"Yeah. Buns and chips, too." Justin closed his eyes, leaned into the car seat.

"Sounds perfect. You okay, babe?"

"Yep."

"Yep?" Chris chuckled. "Your swim tire you out?"

"Hmm? No. No, I don't think so. I'm just resting my eyes."

"Head bothering you?" It had been a long time since he'd seen Justin with a migraine. He didn't like it. Justin no doubt didn't like it even more.

"Not really. I mean, you know how the day or three after anything sets one off? I don't want another one."

"No, I'd rather you avoid getting anymore of them."

"Me too. I think there must have been MSG in the stuff we had for lunch."

"Another reason to make our own."

"It was that fund raiser thing for the kids."

"Huh. Okay, we'll have to look more closely into caterers then." He shot Justin a look. "I'm not risking you."

Justin pinked, but smiled. "I'm just an assistant coach."

"You're an Olympian. You're my lover. And my assistant coach." And maybe more.

"You're my best friend."

He smiled at Justin. "Thank you."

Justin, eyes still closed, reached over and squeezed his leg. "It's true."

"I'm glad." It was important to him that he was a positive influence in Justin's life. A good thing beyond being Justin's coach. And lover. Okay, so he wanted it all.

"Me, too. It's Friday. Do you have plans for the weekend?"

"I thought I'd take you for lunch at the Sliver Lining tomorrow." He wanted to introduce Justin to other people who lived the lifestyle. So Justin didn't feel quite so isolated, so much like he was different.

"Yeah? Okay. Is that a bar?"

"It's a club for people in the lifestyle."

"And anyone can come in?"

"No, you need to be a member."

"Oh. You're a member." Justin's eyes opened. "But you aren't doing lifestyle things with them, right?"

"No, babe. I'm doing lifestyle things with you."

"Okay. I just want to make sure that's clear."

He grinned. "Are you staking your claim, babe?"

"Yes." That was sure.

"I think I like that. A lot."

Justin squeezed his fingers.

"It goes both ways, too."

"Yeah? You aren't going to let anyone try and touch me?" Justin asked.

"That's right." Chris couldn't help the growl in his voice. Nobody was touching Justin. Ever. From any lifestyle.

"Good. I only want you."

"That's good because you're mine. Which doesn't mean I don't want to show you off, introduce you to the guys I know. I'm proud of you, babe."

They turned into the drive and he hit the button for the garage door opener. Justin nodded, and they sat there for a long minute, then Justin headed in. He shook his head, grabbing his sports bag and following that amazing ass. His boy was complex and, while it was fascinating, it could be frustrating as fuck.

At least Justin was happy now, back on a routine, with someone who loved him. There'd been no more drinking, no more talk of crazy stunts that were stupid at best, suicidal at worst. There was something, though, a restlessness. A sense of loss that just never went away. He had a hunch competing again would make a difference to that. He also needed Justin to completely bare his soul, let Chris see everything.

It was the weekend, though, and Chris thought they could explore, stretch. Push. Maybe he just hadn't made up for the time they'd been apart yet. Of course going to Silver Linings with Justin maybe wasn't in the cards yet. If he was going to compete again it might be best for Justin to have no associations with a BDSM club...

Justin was in the kitchen, radio blaring, back door open. He grabbed the dishes from the cupboard, the utensils and went to set the little patio table out back. The hot dogs went on the grill, Justin moving like he was a million miles away.

"Penny for 'em."

"Huh?" Justin looked at him.

"A penny. For your thoughts."

"I'm not thinking. Just making hot dogs."

Uh-huh. "You were a million miles away."

"I'm just thinking about swimming, I guess."

"Yeah? What about swimming?"

"Just that... I don't know if I'm going to be a good coach."

Justin was conscientious, seemed to honestly like the kids, and knew what competitive swimming entailed. Chris thought his babe was immanently qualified. "What's got you worried?"

"It's not what I'm meant to do, I don't think."

Chris bit the inside of his lip to keep from grinning. No, Justin wasn't meant to *coach* swimming. He was purely meant to swim. "No?" He spoke softly, inviting Justin to expand on that thought.

"No. I. I like the kids, though. They're cool." Justin turned the hot dogs. "They're almost done. You want your bun grilled?"

"Yes, please. And the kids are cool. So what do you think you're meant to be doing, then, if not coaching?"

"I think I've already done it."

"Already done what?" Like he didn't know. He could play coy, though, when he wanted to.

"I'm a swimmer. That's what I do. Did. Whatever." His plate was handed to him. "Hot dogs."

He waited until Justin looked up and met his eyes. "It's what you *do*, babe."

"Yeah. Yeah, but it's not like a job, huh? I hoped that the coaching would do it, but it doesn't. I'm sorry."

"So maybe you need to think about swimming again." He took his plate and sat at the table, putting mustard and relish on his dogs.

"I'm retired." Justin took mustard, but didn't eat, just moved the food around listlessly.

"You wouldn't be the first swimmer to come out of

retirement." There was more than three years left for training before the next Olympics, Justin wouldn't even need that long, but he could have it, he could take it.

"I'm too old." Still those long fingers stopped.

He snorted. "How old was it Dara Torres was when she won three silver medals at the Olympics? Younger than you, I guess. Oh, no, she was forty-one at the time."

"I made a mistake, retiring."

That's right. Justin had. "So, unmake it."

"I don't know if I can. I don't know if I know how." Justin chewed his bottom lip. "Maybe. Let's talk about it later."

"One last word and then we *both* eat. You can do anything you want, Justin. I believe in you."

"I know." Justin offered him a half-grin, a nod, but Chris wasn't sure his boy believed him.

It made him want to growl and tie Justin up until he *knew* Justin believed, and stopped giving up on his own life.

He ate, watching Justin pretend to eat, to be present. He growled softly. "How're your hot dogs?"

"Okay. Were yours okay?"

"They were fine. I actually ate them."

"What?" Oh, there. There was a hint of attention.

"You're moping, babe. And I don't think you took more than two bites of your hot dogs."

"I'm not moping." Justin stood up, gathered the plates and the mostly uneaten bag of chips.

"You aren't eating."

"I'm not hungry, I guess."

"You swam forever, you should be starving." He wasn't going to let it go, he was going to keep pushing.

"Let it go, Coach." God, how many thousand times had he heard those words?

"Has that *ever* worked for you?"

"Couple times, maybe." The stubborn set of Justin's lips was hot as hell.

"I don't think even that many." He got up and walked toward Justin, let his love and care for his babe show through as he stalked the man.

"I'm going to..." Justin headed inside, put the dishes down.

He followed. "You're going to what?"

"I don't know. Maybe play a video game or something. Maybe jog."

"I have a much better idea, babe."

"Yeah?"

God, he wanted to tear Justin up. "Yeah." He tugged Justin in close, bringing Justin up against his body.

"Hey. I was going to..."

"Play video games? Get fucked by your sexy lover? Which one would you rather do?"

Justin's smile grew, brushed his lips. "You're better than any video games, Coach."

"I wasn't fishing." Not really.

"Well, it's true. I'm in a weird mood, but it's not about you."

"I'm here to turn weird moods into wild, happy-making sex."

"Wild, happy-making sex, huh?" That earned him a grin. "Okay, I'm in."

"Good." He leaned in to lap at Justin's lips, to bite at the bottom one.

Justin kissed him, still a little distracted, still a little unfocused. He bit Justin's lower lip, not hard, just enough to bring Justin's focus front and center, on him.

"Hey." Justin stepped closer.

"I'm right here, babe." He slid his hands to Justin's waist, tugging the t-shirt out of Justin's jeans.

"I know. I'm sorry. Maybe it's not a good time. Maybe

I'm just stupid today."

"Stop it. You know you're not allowed to talk about yourself like that." In fact it made his voice growly and he smacked Justin's ass.

"Hey! No spanking!"

"Then don't run yourself down." It was simple and Justin knew it.

"Just... People have stupid days. People have worries. I have worries. I'm going to take a shower."

"No, we're going to make love, remember? Wild, happy-making sex."

"Are you going to be pissed if I don't get happy?"

"I'm going to keep trying until you do."

Justin shook his head. "You are stubborn."

He nodded his head. "More stubborn than you and that's saying something."

"Can you... do you think you can make it better?"

He looped his arms around Justin, rubbing his babe's spine. "Is it better now than it was when you first called me?"

"Yes. I... I was close to being really stupid."

"I know. Thank god you called. My point, though, is that I've already made it better, so yes, I think I can make it even better."

"Confident bastard."

"Yep. I know you, babe."

"You think so?" Justin rested one cheek against his shoulder.

"I do. I know you better than anyone else in the whole world." He kept touching, rubbing, adoring his boy. He massaged the lovely ass, and dragged his fingers up along Justin's spine. Justin relaxed for him, leaned into him. He pressed a kiss to Justin's forehead.

"I could stay like this forever."

"Nah, you'd miss the water."

"Maybe."

He snorted. Right. "If we could figure out how to stay in the pool full-time without turning into giant prunes? Then we'd be golden."

"That would be fucking cool, wouldn't it?"

"My water baby." He rubbed them together and figured they had far too many clothes on. Maybe a shower was just the thing, but for both of them. "Bathroom," he murmured. "We can at least manage wet until we're giant prunes."

"See? I told you a shower was good."

He chuckled and nodded, started walking down the hall without letting go of his babe. Justin stayed close and they stayed skin-to-skin as they worked clothes open. He kept kissing and nuzzling as they undressed, not letting Justin lose focus. Then he eased his boy into the water, into the warm spray. Something about the water always eased Justin. It was kind of amazing.

"Reach up, Just. Hold onto the showerhead."

Justin arched, reached up.

They needed some toys for the shower. A hook, attachments for the showerhead. He slid his hand over Justin's water-slick skin. God, he could clean Justin out. His boy would flip out. Just the thought had him hard and he rubbed against Justin's belly.

Justin chuckled. "So horny."

"You make me need, Justin. Make me so hungry."

"I fed you." Little tease.

"Not that kind of hunger, babe. And you know it." He let his words growl and moved in, taking Justin's mouth.

Chris kissed Justin like it was the first time, like it was going to be the only time, fucking those needy, sweet lips. His hands slid down, finding his babe's beautiful, perfect ass. He felt the muscles jerk, roll. It made him squeeze harder.

"Going to drive you crazy this weekend. Going to make it so you just focus on your body, your pleasure." He was going to take Justin out of his head. No thinking, just feeling for two whole days. It was going to be fantastic.

Then, after, they could take about what Justin needed. Really talk. He scraped his nails over Justin's nipples, wanting to make the sensation spark.

Justin shivered, pulled back. "They ache."

"Good." Leaning in, he took one in his mouth and began to suck.

Justin's fingers tangled in his hair, holding onto him. He didn't think Justin knew whether to pull closer or away. They were already slightly swollen of course, but less so now at the end of the day than they were in the morning. He flicked his tongue back and forth across the hard little tip and sucked even harder. His hands slid around Justin's waist, circling it and stroking along Justin's spine.

"Oh, God. Coach..." Justin arched, pushed into his lips.

He nodded, but didn't let go, didn't stop. He kept stroking Justin's skin, too. He wanted this to go on and on. He wanted Justin to need him more than anything else in life, because god knew he felt that way about his lover. More and more every day. "Love these sweet nubs."

"You're obsessed." Justin petted his temple.

"There are worse things to be obsessed with."

"Swimming. Stats. Uh... potatoes."

He looked at Justin and one eyebrow went up. "Potatoes?"

Justin shrugged, grinned.

"Are you trying to tell me something? Is there a French fry or mashed fetish I should be aware of?"

Justin's laughter rang out, and he fell in love, that little bit more.

"I hope that's a no." He gave those sweet tits a last

pinch, then let his hands drift down to Justin's ass. "Of course, I'm pretty obsessed about this, too."

"You are. It feels good, having you want me."

"Good." Thank god Justin recognized that.

"Can we...Can you take me to bed?"

"That's where we're headed, babe." He kissed Justin's nose and started moving them in that direction down the hall.

"No. I know that. I mean, can we... I need to not think."

"Oh, good boy." For Justin to recognize his need and to verbalize it, ask for it.

He kissed Justin hard. Justin melted into him, clinging to him, lips open and eager. He grabbed Justin's ass, lifting his lover up and against himself as he kept moving. Justin wrapped around him, holding on, trusting in his strength.

He got them to the bedroom and leaned over, falling onto the bed, onto Justin. Justin oofed, still laughing, then squeezed him. He pressed kisses all over Justin's face, their bodies rocking gently, rubbing them together. He warmed Justin up, enjoying the sensations of his boy underneath him.

"Want to bind you, babe. Stretch you out and clamp your nipples, bind your prick and warm your skin with my hand."

"Please. I just want to feel today. My brain is sore."

Then what he had planned would be perfect.

He tugged on one of Justin's nipples, leaving it stinging as he got up and went to the drawer where he had the stuff he needed. Justin curled up around a pillow, watching him. He grabbed the nipple clamps and a cock ring, and then found some silk rope. He grabbed four hanks so he could bind Justin spread eagle. Then he found a paddle, a nice plug for after they made love. So he could leave his spunk inside Justin's body. Shit, just the thought made him groan.

"You look happy." Justin was holding the pillow like a lover.

He brought the stuff over and set it on the bed next to Justin. "That's because I am. You make me happy, babe."

"Good." Justin's eyes looked over the toys, but his lover didn't say anything.

"You want to know what these things are and what I'm going to do with them?"

"I know what they are, but... it would be incredibly hot, to hear you tell what you're going to do."

"Yeah, it would be, wouldn't it?" He grinned at Justin.

"Uh-huh." Justin grinned back, still curled into the pillow.

"These are nipple clamps and I'm gong to use them to bite at your nipples, to pinch them."

"My poor nipples."

"You're going to love it." He truly believed Justin would.

"I'll trust you, Coach." Justin rubbed one cheek against the pillow, stubble rasping.

He stroked the other cheek. "Good, babe."

Chris wrapped a hank of rope around one of Justin's wrists. "I want you spread-eagle." He tied the other end of the rope to the top right corner of the bed, then he wrapped the other wrist. "I want you all stretched out for me."

Justin let him bind those strong arms before testing the bonds.

"Ready for me to do your ankles, babe?"

"I guess? You won't leave me in here like this, right?"

"I thought you said you were going to trust me, babe?"

"I do. I do, I'm just... It's a little scary."

"I'm not going to leave you here. I'm going to be right here with you." He would never have thought that the idea of being left bound was scary for Justin. Chris leaned in and whispered into Justin's ear. "I wouldn't miss a second of you bound and spread for me."

Justin relaxed, sighing softly as he sank into the mattress.

"Fuck, you're beautiful, Justin. You steal my breath."

"I wish."

"No need to wish because you do."

Justin's legs spread, ankles reaching for the bonds, offering him that sweet submission. Moaning, he wrapped his hand around Justin's right ankle, slowly wrapping the rope around it. His lover, his boy was giving this to him, offering it easily. He was so hard, just from this.

He touched Justin's foot, caressed it as he pulled the other end of the rope and tied it around the bottom poster. That left one foot, waiting for him, Justin's heavy muscles jerking and twitching just enough to be visible. Bending, he kissed the calf of Justin's free leg, and the moved to kiss the ankle, warming it in his hand before he tied the rope around it.

Justin's cock was flagging, just a bit, proving his lover's nerves.

He got that last limb bound, and then settled on his knees between Justin's legs, his hands dragging gently up from ankles to knees to soft inner thighs. "You're all fuzzy."

Justin chuckled. "I know, right? It's taken forever to get used to."

"I imagine we can have fun shaving you. And imagine how this'll feel without all those little hairs."

"I don't know. I'm not competing."

"Doesn't mean we can't do it for fun." Besides, he didn't believe Justin wasn't going to un-retire. Not for a second.

"True." Justin chuckled. "If it's gone, you can't tug it."

"You mean like this?" He tugged, softly, and then harder, winking.

"Y...yes! Turkey!"

He laughed, tugging again, though not hard now. There was nothing like this—this simple happiness. Bending, he put a kiss on Justin's belly, licked around the dent of Justin's navel. He loved the sound of the soft, deep hum.

Licking his way down, he felt Justin's prick filling again, nudging at his chin. Hungry man. He rubbed his cheek against the tip, encouraging blood to flow. He rolled Justin's balls with one hand, reached up for one of those pretty nipples with the other. Justin's hips pushed up, making him fight for it.

He flicked his tongue across the tip of Justin's prick. Justin arched higher, but only for a second, like the man was digging into the water. He groaned, taking the head of Justin's cock into his mouth and sucking eagerly. Justin cried out and then his boy was fucking his lips, body using the ropes for leverage.

Grabbing the cockring, he let Justin chase his pleasure for a few moments before pulling off. He wrapped his boy up quickly, trapping his lover.

"Coach!"

"Yes, babe?" He smiled at Justin like butter wouldn't melt in his mouth.

"Love you."

Oh, fuck. He leaned up and took Justin's mouth. His hands cradled Justin's cheeks, holding his lover still as he plundered the man's mouth. "I love you, babe. Really."

"Good." Justin moaned, chasing his lips. "Less talking, more kissing."

"I still have nipple clamps to apply."

"Kissing. You're supposed to be kissing."

"No, I'm supposed to be blowing your mind."

"Supposed to be."

"Oh, sass!" His hand landed on the side of Justin's ass, the smack firm, but not harsh. He hit it again, though, and then again. Loving the way each smack made Justin catch his breath. His sweet boy. He spanked the inside of Justin's thighs. He loved the way they pinked up for him.

"Burns. Fuck, Chris. Coach."

"Sweet boy." He scraped his nails along the pretty thighs.

Justin cried out, pulling at the cuffs, and he shook his head. No straining the shoulders. There'd been too much work done on them to screw them up now with this.

"I don't mind if you forget and accidentally tug at them, but once you remember they're there, no pulling. They're to hold you, not strain your muscles."

"What does it matter?"

Because you're a swimmer and you could do damage if you pull with all your strength." He was almost scandalized that Justin hadn't put that together himself.

"I'm not a swimmer anymore." Justin sighed. "Still, I'd be miserable if I couldn't get into the pool, so you're right."

"I'm always right, babe."

"Mostly right."

He chuckled. "Nitpicker."

"No lice for me."

Okay. Okay, Justin was altogether too coherent. He flicked his boy's nipples. Justin's pecs jerked, tensed. That was better. He rubbed them with his thumbs. Swollen and hard, they responded to his touch, almost reaching for his fingers. Groaning he grabbed for the clamps.

"Please." Justin's lips chased his.

He didn't kiss Justin, though; he flicked the right nipple, and then clamped it.

"No. No, fuck." Justin jerked, pulled the cuffs. "Take it off."

"I don't think so, babe. I have a second one to put on." And now he had Justin's full attention.

"Please. It aches. Fuck." Justin tried to kick, tried to get free.

He pinched the other nipple and then slipped the clamp on.

"Fuck..." Justin panted, cheeks red. "Oh, fuck."

He stroked Justin's belly. "Breathe through it, babe. Push through the pain."

Chris watched Justin struggle, his babe so beautiful, so right there in his own skin. The only other time Justin was like this was in the water.

"Why are you doing this?" Justin knew. Chris knew that. Justin had asked for this.

"Because it's what you want. What you need." Chris stroked the bound prick.

"I don't." Justin's body began to relax, to accept.

"You do, babe." He rubbed alongside Justin's prick, then rolled the tight little balls. He tapped behind Justin's balls, pushing just a little too hard. He loved the way Justin arched for him, moaned. "Sweet boy." He pushed again, and again.

Reaching up, he flicked the clamp on Justin's right nipple. Justin tugged, trying to pull away from him.

"There's nowhere to go, babe."

Justin didn't answer him, just jerked again. He touched the clamp on the left nipple next.

"You're going to feel bad when they fall off."

That had him laughing and he bent to lick around the left nipple. "You're right—I will. If they do."

"They will. Poor abused bits." God, Justin was in a wild mood.

"You love that I keep them red and swollen and full." He flicked both at the same time.

"Do not."

Chris snorted, flicked the clamps harder this time.

"Ow! Stop it." Justin groaned. "God, you make me whiny."

That had him chuckling. "You're not feeling enough."

"Coach, stop. Just leave them alone for a minute."

"No, I don't think so." He rubbed the tip of Justin's prick with his palm, his other hand sliding around Justin's nipples and randomly nudging the clamps.

"Please? Come on, they ache."

Chris leaned in and wrapped his mouth around Justin's right nipple, breathing heat on the swollen, trapped flesh. The clamps weren't vicious, they were firm and on the sensitive tits, they'd be intense, but not truly painful. He licked around Justin's nipple, then touched the clamp with his tongue. Justin groaned, shivered for him.

He licked again, his hand moving to cup Justin's balls, to stroke them. The sweet velvety sac drew up, wrinkled against his palm. He loved the feeling of them, the way touching them like this made Justin moan with need. He stroked behind the sweet sac, keeping the touch feather light.

Justin's skin was so hot here, and smooth as anything. Groaning, he slipped his fingers back further. He pinched the skin there, lightly. "When you win your next medal, I'm going to pierce you here, with a tiny, tiny ring."

"What?"

"You heard me, babe." He pinched again.

"I'm not competing anymore."

"Uh-huh." Justin would come out of retirement, he was more sure of it every day his babe got in the pool.

"I'm not."

"Because you hate swimming so much." He flicked Justin's right nipple, clamp and all, with his tongue.

"Love it. Fuck!"

"I know, Justin. That's why you need to go back to it.

You *need* it." Swimming was like breathing for his boy. You couldn't live without breathing.

"I can't. I quit."

"So un-quit."

"Does it work that... why are we talking?"

"We're talking?" He stroked his fingers over Justin's hole. "And yes. It works that way."

"I want it to."

"It does." He kept stroking Justin's wrinkled, hot hole.

"Feels good. No more talking."

"Bossy boy."

"Bossy would be to say 'now'." Oh, Justin was feeling better.

He laughed. "I believe you just did." He leaned in and flicked one nipple clamp with his tongue, setting it moving as he pushed a finger into Justin's tight little hole.

Justin moaned, lips parting for him as the muscles squeezed his fingers. He leaned up and took a kiss, tongue fucking Justin's mouth as his finger fucked Justin's hole. Hot, needy boy. The tight hole rippled around his touch, holding him. Groaning, he pushed his finger deeper, wanting to hit that spot inside Justin, make his babe crazy. When he hit it, Justin cried out, jerked and tugged the bonds. Of course, that had him hitting it again, then again.

"Coach. Coach!"

Uh-huh. Right there. He was on it. He flicked at the tip of Justin's cock with his free hand, then at the right nipple clamp again.

"Take them off. Please."

"It's going to hurt worse when I do."

"Evil·man. Always hurting me."

"Like you don't love the way it makes you feel."

Justin shook his head, moaned low.

"You can come when I do it." He leaned in and

grabbed the right clamp, undoing it.

Justin's face went slack, muscles jerking on the bonds.

"Let go and come for me, babe." He took the other clamp off.

"Oh, God." Justin sobbed and he stroked a single line, from nipple to hip, drawing Justin's come from him.

He stroked Justin's balls, encouraging aftershocks. Justin cried out, muttering for him, shaking. Leaning in, he began to lick the come from his boy's belly. Bitter and salty, the flavor exploded on his tongue. Groaning, he kept licking, lapping at Justin's skin, the flavor of chlorine and Justin himself there beneath the saltiness of the come.

"Coach. Coach, your tongue's so hot."

"Uh-huh." He kept licking, kept cleaning the smooth, supple flesh. He wanted to lose himself in this, in his sweet lover. He nibbled his way over to Justin's cock, licking at the tip. "When you win another Olympic gold, we're piercing this."

Justin groaned.

"This," he leaned in and licked at the spot behind Justin's balls. "Is for your first world medal. Up to you whether it's next year or the year after."

"Coach..."

That was right. He was. "You better believe it." He bit the base of Justin's sac, tugging with his teeth. Then he lapped the sensitive orbs, humming as he wet them. They drew up, tight and hard. Sweet boy. He nudged them with his nose, and then slapped them with his tongue.

"H...hey." Justin groaned, toes curling. "Don't."

He did it again.

"Coach! Don't."

So of course, he did it again, tongue hitting the sensitive orbs.

"Tell me it's going to be okay, everything."

He gave off playing with Justin's balls, moving instead

Golden

to rub his cheek against the long, hard prick. "It's all going to be okay, babe. Everything. But most of all you and me."

"I believe you." Justin nodded. "I do."

"Good. Because it's true." He took the tip of Justin's prick in and sucked gently.

"Love that..." Justin moaned.

He sucked harder.

"Yes. God, yes." Sensitive, needy boy.

Chris slid his fingers back and rubbed at Justin's hole. He found a rhythm—tongue fucking that tiny slit, fingers fucking the tight hole. Justin soon had it, too, hips moving with him, low sounds coming from his babe and going straight to his balls. It was like dancing, like swimming.

Groaning, he moved faster, bringing everything up a notch. He added another finger, spreading Justin a little wider. So fucking tight. He wanted to bury himself in Justin and fuck that sweet hole 'til kingdom come.

"Need." Justin pulled at the bonds. "Fuck."

"I'll give you what you need, babe. When I decide to."

Justin groaned, fighting a little.

"Fight as much as you need to, babe. That's why you're tied to my bed."

"Are you going to let me go?"

"Of course. When we're done."

"You're never done with me." Justin had a point.

"No, and I never will be." He smiled at Just. "And if you extrapolate from that, you know it means I'll never let you go."

"Is it cool if that makes me feel good?"

"It's extremely cool." He loved it.

"It does. Make me feel good, I mean."

He licked from the base of Justin's prick to the tip, grinning. "Good." His lips twitched.

"Good-good." Justin grinned wide.

194

He laughed, tickling Justin's ribs.

"So mean to me!" Justin was laughing harder.

"The meanest coach in the history of the world."

"Yes! Evil!"

Laughing, he pressed his mouth to the inside of Justin's thigh and blew. Justin snorted, cock bobbing on the flat belly.

"This is supposed to be kinky, sexy," he pointed out, tongue tickling the same skin he'd raspberried a moment ago.

"It's fun. I feel fun."

He smiled against Justin's skin. "Excellent." He was pretty sure Justin hadn't had a lot of fun since his retirement.

"It is. It so totally is, Coach."

He nodded and ran his hands over whatever skin he could touch, loving on his babe.

"This is crazy. I never thought, when we were together before, that you were in to things like this."

"It was my job to keep this and you separate." It had been the hardest thing ever, not letting Justin know how he felt, what he wanted. Especially when Justin had retired and he'd let the love of his life leave to find his own way in the world.

"I'm glad I'm not your job anymore."

"Me, too." He licked up along Justin's cock. "Though you're older now, and we started this first, so if you wanted to go back to it..." He wouldn't be taking advantage of his swimmer if they were lovers before Justin went back to swimming. Which they were. He licked his way down again.

"H...huh?" Justin groaned, rolled for him.

He didn't say it again, he just lost himself in the scent and flavors of Justin's sweet flesh. Justin let him—offering him moans and soft cries, the periodic jingle of the chains delicious. He moved down to lick at Justin's hole again. He wanted Just, needed to be buried deep inside.

"Fuck, that's so hot. So hot, Coach. Love. Please."

He pushed his tongue in, fucking Justin with it. Justin groaned, body fighting to get closer. He was in charge, though, he dictated how far his tongue went, what pleasure Justin could have. He slowed even further, loving the desperate sounds. His fingers slid over Justin's balls, feeling the heat of them, the tightness.

"Need you. Need you, Coach."

"You got me, babe."

Justin so did.

"I'm feeling so fluttery inside."

"Enjoy it, Justin."

Justin moaned, muscles rippling. "I'm trying."

He increased the speed of his tongue-fucking, making sure he got Justin nice and wet. Justin cried out, thighs trembling violently. He slid his tongue out of Justin's hole and surged up, pressing his cock in its place.

"Yes!" Justin jerked, bucking against him.

"Needy boy." He pulled out and slammed back in again.

"Yes. Yes, I need. Please. More."

"Yes. More." He continued to rock, to push in and fill his babe.

Justin grabbed hold of the headboard, the cuffs twisting around his swimmer's wrists. He held Justin's gaze as he fucked his babe, keeping them connected mind and body. Justin's eyes were heavy-lidded, unfocused. That was what he wanted, to drive Justin into a place of feeling, of pleasure.

He kept his rhythm going, biting on his lower lip to hold it there. Justin's body was like a vice, muscles rippling around him, jerking violently. His boy would need to come soon, wouldn't be able to hold back despite the cock ring. He was pushing a little longer, though, riding this bliss just a few more thrusts.

"Wait for it, boy. Hold on."

"Trying."

"Try harder." He shifted, deliberately hitting Justin's gland on the next thrust—he wanted Justin to have to work for it, to work to obey him.

"Fuck!" Justin's body squeezed him hard.

Barely holding on, he pushed in twice more hitting Justin's gland. Then he shouted. "Come, babe. Now!"

Justin sobbed, jerking underneath him, seed spraying over the flat belly. His own come pushed out of him, filling Justin. He hadn't even finished coming when he reached for the heavy plug.

"Gonna lock myself in you, babe."

"Huh?" Justin blinked, obviously dazed.

"I'm going to plug you, with my seed inside you."

"Oh..." Oh, someone liked the sound of that.

"That's right." He stayed buried for long enough to kiss Justin long and hard, and then began to slip out, plug at the ready.

Justin's body fought him, squeezed him.

Groaning, he pressed their foreheads together. "So good, babe."

"Uh. Uh-huh."

"Gotta let me come out now." He pushed back in, nudging Justin's gland again.

"Uhn." Justin's eyes crossed.

He slowly began to pull out once more.

"Coach. Coach, I need you."

He pushed back in again. "Got me."

"Yes..." The look of need on Justin's face was delicious.

He thrust again, then again. Justin accepted him, taking him in and in, crying out for him. Groaning, he kept thrusting, lost again in the pleasure of their bodies.

Fuck, Justin made him feel like a superhero. He kept moving, building them back up. Justin was moaning, jerking, bound cock slapping that pretty belly.

"Yeah, that's it, babe. Show me how good it is."

Justin just nodded, lips open and needy. Leaning in, he changed his angle slightly and kissed those lips, tracing them with his tongue first before making it a real kiss. Justin groaned, tongue fucking his lips. He nipped at Justin's tongue and then sucked on it, soothing the little hurt. He felt Justin's joy, milking his cock.

He undid the cockring and slipped it off; Justin could have this second orgasm as soon as he wanted it.

"Love you. Oh, fuck. Coach."

"Love you, babe. Show me. Come for me. Come on." He slammed in again.

Justin sobbed, fighting to shoot, caught up. He slid his hand down and rubbed a finger over Justin's slit. When he let his nail dig in, Justin lost it, screaming and shooting for him. He let go as well, more of his spunk filing Justin's body.

This time he didn't wait, he slipped free and plugged Justin while his boy was still moaning. He turned the plug until it was perfectly seated. Then he stroked Justin's belly, rubbing his boy's spunk into the fine belly.

"Oh, god. So much."

"Just enough." He kissed Justin's belly and then the lovely lips.

"Uh-huh. Enough."

"Ready to be undone, babe?"

"Uh-huh."

He kissed his way up to Justin's right wrist. Justin's fingers curled, his boy relaxed, easy. He massaged Justin's wrist, his arm, and then moved to kiss his way up the other arm. As soon as Justin's arms were free, Justin grabbed him, held him. He kissed his boy, moaning into

Justin's mouth as his lover held on.

"The plug, Chris."

"No, you mean the cuffs around your ankles have to come off." The plug was staying. He could tell that Justin was working the plug, body moving around it. "That stays in, boy."

"How long?" Justin's hips were already moving again.

"Until morning."

"I'll go crazy."

"I'll hold you through it."

"Promise?"

"I swear."

His sweet, loving boy melted for him, nodded. "Thank you."

"Always." He got Justin's legs free of the cuffs and then tugged Just into his arms, ready to hold Justin all night long. Hell, he was ready to hold Justin forever.

"Love." Justin sighed, long and slow.

"Yeah, babe. Love you forever."

"Forever sounds perfect. I need some sleep. My head's full of thoughts."

That made him chuckle. "God forbid."

"I know, right?"

He laughed and kissed Justin through it. God, he was never letting go of Justin again.

Chapter Sixteen

Chris had errands to run and the kids weren't in the pool, so Justin went to do laps. He worked the water, just moving and turning, pushing himself fast for a few laps, then taking a dozen laps slow and lazy before speeding along again. This was where he needed to be. Right here, cutting through the water.

"So un-resign." Coach's voice rang in his head.

I can't, Coach, he thought. *What if I've lost it? What if I'm not good anymore?*

He swore he could hear Coach snort and threaten to spank him if he kept running himself down.

Creepy.

Also, it sort of made him smile.

He heard someone jump into the water. He stopped at the edge, looking over, arms tired enough that they felt like they weighed a thousand pounds.

Coach grinned at him. "I'm all erranded out. You gonna be much longer here?"

"I was just goofing off." Coach would growl, if he knew how long Justin had actually been going.

Coach chuckled. "You ready to call it a day, then? I need to do a few laps to keep my tummy down."

"I can do more." Maybe. He headed off, his muscles totally shot, his form blown to hell.

They swam a few laps and then Coach stopped him. "I

thought you said you'd just been goofing off?"

"Uh-huh." His heart raced, pounding in his chest.

"For how long?"

"Huh?" Fuck.

"Get out of the pool, Justin. You know better than to overwork yourself."

"I'm good." He wasn't training.

Coach climbed out and held out a hand to him, one eyebrow raised. He looked at Coach's hand, trying to force his arm to raise, but it wouldn't go.

"Justin..." Coach shook his head, leaned down and grabbed him under the arms, dragging him out of the water.

"Thanks." He landed on the coping, his ass slapping on the tile.

"Damn it, babe. You know better than this."

"I was just playing around."

"No, playing around doesn't leave you too tired to stand or to pull yourself out of the pool. What if I hadn't come along when I did?"

"I'm okay! Don't snarl! You're not my coach anymore, right?"

"I'm your lover and that gives me every right to be worried about you drowning yourself. And if you're so okay, let's see you get up."

"I won't drown!" He pulled his legs up, stood, and rolled his eyes. "See?" Then his left leg collapsed and he went crashing into the water.

"Justin!" He heard Coach's shout, the splash as Coach jumped in.

He didn't panic—the water was his home, but his arms didn't want to pull him more than a stroke or two.

Coach came up from beneath him, pulling him back against the solid body. "I've got you."

"I hit my leg on the coping, Coach." He knew better than to struggle.

"You're okay. I've got you."

He nodded. "Am I in trouble?"

Coach swam them to the edge and pushed him up over onto the edge of the pool. "Let's get you out and make sure you're okay first."

"Okay." They got him back up, his leg already bruising.

Coach rubbed his other leg, his arms. "How are you feeling?"

"Stupid."

Coach nodded. "You know better."

"I was thinking."

"Proving yet again how dangerous that is." Coach winked.

"Yeah, yeah." He closed his eyes, counting to twenty as the room spun.

"What's wrong?"

"Just a little dizzy."

Coach growled at him.

"What?"

"I don't like it when you're hurt, babe. Especially when it was something avoidable."

"I just needed to swim it out."

Coach just looked at him. He sighed.

"Come on, babe. Showers and then home."

"Uh-huh." He sat up, testing his sore, sore leg.

"How bad is it?"

"Tender. Not broken, I don't think."

"Good." Coach helped him stand, arm around his waist as they started moving.

He moved, made it to the showers before he needed to sit again. Coach cleaned him as he sat in the stall, water falling all around him.

"I'm okay." He was going to die before he got home.

"Don't try to fudge the truth with me."

"You're coaching again."

"You think if I had never coached, I wouldn't care that you're pushing yourself and dancing around the truth with me?"

"If you'd never coached. That's like saying, if the sun stopped rising."

"Then you can't expect me not to be coach." Coach gave him a wink.

"I don't. I mean I expect you to be the coach. I just, you don't have to be."

"I love you, babe. Call it coaching, call it caring for my lover, call it what you want, it's what I do and I'm not going to stop."

"Love you." He held on, breathing slow. "We should go home."

"You think you can walk yet?"

"I can. I'm hungry."

"I'll bet. You want hot dogs? We got some. Buns even, I think."

"Oh, yum. You know I love hot dogs."

"You love anything I cook instead of you."

"Don't be ugly. I was paying you a compliment." He cooked, didn't he? All the fucking time. And he was good at it.

"I wasn't being ugly!"

"You were, too. You act like I'm this spoiled brat, and I'm not. I work hard."

"I do not treat you like a spoiled brat, and I know you work hard. Aren't you in trouble in fact for working too hard in the pool?" Coach grabbed his arms and pulled him up against the solid body, eyes staring right into his. "What's this about, Justin?"

"I want to compete again. I don't want to teach kids how to do this. I want to race." The words poured out of him in a rush.

Coach's lips spread into a smile that reached his eyes. "Done."

"Yeah?"

"You bet. I'll call the national body and tell them you're training for next year's world's."

"Okay. Okay, yeah." His heart was racing.

Coach wrapped around him, hugging him hard. "I'm proud of you, Justin. So fucking proud."

"I want to go home and just... be home."

"You're always home when we're together." Coach turned off the water and grabbed a towel, started to dry him down.

"Yeah. It's been a rough day."

"I've got you, babe." Coach kissed his forehead.

"I know." It meant the world to him.

"Then let's go home and have hot dogs. We have a comeback to plan."

"Okay. Yes. Let's get to work."

Coach's arm went around his shoulders, leading him back to the locker room and his clothes. Yeah. They had work to do.

It felt good.

They had hot dogs with mustard and sauerkraut, and washed them down with water. They were going to have to set up a meal plan as well as a training plan. Chris had to admit, he was looking forward to having a swimmer in contention again.

They cleaned up together and he bumped hips with his babe.

"I'm going to go take an Advil, Coach. I'm sore, all over."

"Go get naked and lie down on the bed, babe."

"Okay." There was a new relaxation in Justin's shoulders, a sense of self.

Chris followed slowly, admiring his boy. "I'm going to give you a massaging. Baby oil and everything."

"Really? I haven't had a full massage from you in years."

"Then it's about time you did."

"I always hated your massages, you know that?"

"You did?" He'd thought Justin had enjoyed them.

"Uh-huh." Justin nodded. "I was always terrified that I'd spring wood."

"Ah, well I promise you that this time I'm going to be disappointed if you don't."

He got a quick grin. "I'll see what I can do."

"Lie on your stomach, babe. We'll start with your back."

He waited until Justin was lying down and then straddled the lovely back. Justin's muscles were overworked and the latent tension was evident in the broad shoulders. He rubbed babe oil over his hands and onto Justin's back, then started rubbing, working the abused muscles. This sound filled the air—pure joy, this deep release. He made a happy noise himself and kept working, making sure he got every muscle relaxed.

Justin was melted underneath him, quiet, still. He worked his way down Justin's back and then rubbed that pretty ass. Those muscled legs spread for him, totally trusting. He massaged his way down Justin's thighs. Justin moaned, legs trembling for him. He rubbed his way back up so he could tease the skin between Justin's balls and his hole.

"Oh..." Justin's hips rolled.

"Feeling better, babe?" He repeated the caress.

"Yes. God, yes."

"Good." He gave Justin's hole one last tickle before

going back to Justin's legs, rubbing the strong calves.

Justin groaned, the sound almost pained.

"These are still sore."

"Yes. Yes, Coach."

"I've got you covered." He kept working Justin's poor leg muscles.

"Oh, God. Oh, God. Sore. Hurts."

"Okay, babe. Just breathe. Breathe through it."

Justin nodded, toes curling, muscles tightening up. He kept working the stubborn muscles, not scolding Justin for pushing today—Justin *knew*; his muscles were telling him every second.

The soft cries told him that they were finding the spot where the massage was going to start working. His boy was going to have to rest tomorrow—completely, totally, and let the muscles heal. He'd have to remind Justin that it wasn't a punishment, it wasn't reneging on the rules: it was simply what happened when these poor muscles were overworked.

Finally Justin let out a storm of sharp curses, a soft sob, and then his muscles let go.

"That's it, babe." Chris gentled his movements, fingers rubbing, easing the loosened muscle.

"Oh, God. Better. Better. Oh, God."

Yeah, he'd bet it was. He rubbed his hands all the way down to Justin's feet, warming and working them as well. Justin was boneless when he turned his boy over. He started at his boy's feet, slowly working his way back up. He didn't mess with the black, awful bruise on Justin's leg. He needed to get ice and heat on that.

He rubbed his thumbs along Justin's hips. His swimmer. His. His no longer retired swimmer.

"Love you, babe."

"Love." Justin's face was a study in peace.

Smiling, he kept the massage going, rubbing Justin's

amazing abs gently. He started working down one arm, paying attention to the man's shoulder. Then he worked his way back up and over to the other side. It was a massage, but it was more now than massages used to be. Now he could enjoy as he touched, could think about it being more.

Justin moaned, soft, low, legs beginning to shift. It was beginning to turn, this massage, from relaxation to sensational. He rubbed his thumbs across Justin's nipples. The sweet rosy nips drew up, reached for his touch.

"Sweet wanton."

"I'm not sweet, am I?" Justin asked.

"The way you need is." He noted that Justin didn't deny the wanton.

"I can accept that." The corners of Justin's lips turned up.

Chuckling, Chris leaned up and kissed that smile. Justin moaned for him, lips chasing his. He pressed them together, taking kiss after kiss.

"Love you, huh?" Justin looked into his eyes.

"I know. And I love you. And everything is going to work out wonderfully."

"You think so?" Justin looked like he couldn't fight his grin.

"No, I *know* so."

"I hope so."

"You hope, I'll know." He wrapped a hand around Justin's prick, "massaging" it.

"Coach. Oh, God. I used to..."

"Used to what, babe?"

"Imagine. Fantasize."

"About this?" He kept stroking the hot, hard flesh.

"Yes. God, yes. About a massage turning into something bigger."

"So I'm your fantasy come true."

"You always have been."

Oh. Oh, damn. Moaning, he kissed Justin until they were both breathless. Justin was holding onto him, rocking against him. He spread Justin's legs with his knees, and Justin spread, wrapping those strong legs around him. He nudged at that sweet little hole.

Justin groaned, shifted his hips so they rubbed together. He kept pushing, the tip of his cock breaching Justin's hole. He moaned as the sweet tightness scraped against his prick.

"Babe.... so tight." He pushed in a little further.

"Deeper." Justin moaned, taking him in deeper and deeper.

He nodded, pushing in harder.

"Chris. Chris, love." Justin looked right at him, eyes burning. "You're the only thing bigger than the water." There was no higher compliment in Justin's world.

"Babe..." He groaned, thrusting in hard.

"Yeah." Justin groaned and kissed him, the need burning him to the core.

Chris started thrusting, pushing into his babe over and over. The sweet body rippled around him, gripping his cock. He found a rhythm, riding Justin's body. It was slow, easy, mind-blowingly sweet.

Taking Justin's lips, he opened them, fucked them with his tongue. Justin fed him sweet cries, low moans. He got a hand around his babe's cock, moving harder now, faster.

"Yes. Yes. Yes." His boy. His lover. He kept fucking, kept jacking, urging his boy to come. He felt the impending orgasm, muscles fluttering around his cock. "Come on, Justin. Come on my cock."

"God, yes. Please."

"Yes." Chris hissed, his own orgasm right there and he needed Justin to come first. He slammed in and Justin arched, heels digging into his thighs. "Come on babe. Come on." He slammed in again, and again.

"Master." The word was bit out for the first time, and then his sweet boy came for him.

"Fuck." He came hard, the word spurring him on.

Justin's body rippled around him, so sweet. He pressed kisses over Justin's cheeks and lips, panting for breath.

"Oh, god." Justin moaned. "So amazing."

"You are, babe."

"Tell me again that we're going to do it."

"I'm calling the head office on Monday, babe. And that's when the real training will begin. Diet, exercise, practice. We're going the whole nine yards."

"Okay. I believe you."

"Good. My gold medal Olympian."

Justin nodded. "Yeah. Yeah, I am."

"You know what the important part of that phrase is, babe?"

"Yours, love."

"That's exactly right." He kissed Justin hard. "You are. Always and forever."

"Then the rest is just..."

They grinned at each other like idiots.

"Golden."

End.

Golden

CPSIA information can be obtained at www.ICGtesting.com
Printed in the USA
BVOW020959190313

315906BV00015B/309/P